D1058629

Also by Judith Caseley

The
Kissing
Diary

The Kissing Diary

Judith Caseley

Frances Foster Books

Farrar, Straus and Giroux • New York

www.fsgkidsbooks.com

Library of Congress Cataloging-in-Publication Data
Caseley, Judith.
    The kissing diary / Judith Caseley.— 1st ed.
        p.   cm.
    Summary: As thirteen-year-old Rosie Goldglitt contemplates
kissing the boy she has a crush on, she tries to navigate the
many complications in her life, including her horrible name,
her nemesis Mary Katz, her parents' divorce, and her mother's
new boyfriend.
    ISBN-13: 978-0-374-36346-8
    ISBN-10: 0-374-36346-3
    [1. Interpersonal relations—Fiction.   2. Schools—Fiction.
3. Divorce—Fiction.   4. Diaries—Fiction.]   I. Title.

PZ7.C2677 Ks 2007
[Fic]—dc22
                                                2006048406

To Jenna,
my shining star

The Kissing

Diary

1

The Diary Rosie Never Wanted

Rosie Goldglitt sat in the corner of the dining room, doing the unmentionable. She was peering through a crack in the door to the living room, watching her mother kiss a strange man on the couch. She wasn't kissing the couch, of course. She was kissing his mouth. He wasn't really a stranger either. His name was Sam, and he was her mother's new boyfriend, if you could call an old man of forty or fifty a boy. Mary Katz, Rosie's worst enemy in the world, wouldn't be caught dead watching her mother kiss a man on the couch. For one thing, her parents weren't divorced. They drove matching Mercedeses and smiled a lot. For another, Mary knew all about kissing, and didn't need to do scientific research on other people. And Mary's couch would be a butter-soft leather sofa that stretched from one end of their mansion to the other.

In the name of science, Rosie squinted and crinkled up her nose as she examined her mother's closed eyes. Did people always shut their eyes to kiss, she wondered. Sam's eyes were closed, too, and one of his hands was moving like a sluggish rodent up and down her mother's back.

Rosie had been thinking a lot about kissing. She even looked up the word in the dictionary. *A touch or caress with the lips as a sign of love, affection, or greeting.* What would it be like to kiss her big crush, Robbie Romano? Could she do it? Would she like it? What if she kissed him and opened her eyes, and he was looking back at her? She shuddered at the thought.

Rosie pressed herself back against the wall. Maybe watching her mother was a bad idea. It made her feel kind of sick. She thought to herself that a new word should be invented that combined being mesmerized and disgusted at the same time. A word that meant "fascinated" as well as "repulsed." *Mesmergusted*, that was it. Or *fascinpulsed*. Whatever you called it, Rosie was stuck in the dining room and couldn't escape upstairs without giving herself away.

It was her mother and father's fault, of course. When they were married, she couldn't remember the last time she had seen them kiss. Kissing had to do with liking a person, didn't it? Maybe that's why she never saw them do it. Her mother obviously liked Sam a lot. Her eyes did this little dance when she talked about him. Rosie obviously liked Robbie if she wanted to plant her lips on his wide mouth, which sometimes had a tiny blemish below. If Rosie were researching the signs of divorce, the absence of kissing would be at the top of the list.

She wanted to run upstairs to record her findings in her diary, the same diary she had chucked in the garbage can when her father had given it to her almost a year ago.

It was a fateful moment. She remembered being on the phone with her best friend, Lauren Jamison, when her father had marched into the living room and said, "Please hang up. I have to talk to you."

"In a minute, Dad," Rosie told him, irritated by the interruption.

"Now," he said, looking so somber that she was afraid he was going to tell her that someone had died.

In the few moments it took to say goodbye to Lauren, Rosie wondered what she'd done wrong. Had she mouthed off disrespectfully to her mother? Not lately. Did she stay too long in the shower that morning, when her father needed the bathroom? Not serious enough. Had a teacher discovered that she'd cheated on a test? Not likely, as Rosie had vowed she'd never do it again when she'd copied Keith's paper in sixth-grade science and her original answer had been right.

Rosie sat opposite her father in the bright yellow kitchen, under the indecipherable clock that had vegetables for numbers. Her brother, Jimmy, would ask her, "Is it eight o'clock yet?" and Rosie would tell him, "It's a quarter past broccoli." The two of them would shriek with laughter while she ran over to the oven clock to read the digital numbers. Her mother would go crazy and say, "What kind of world do we live in where children can't tell time?"

Her father didn't look as though he was going to discuss the problem arising from digital clocks. Rosie couldn't help noticing a package wrapped in brown paper sitting on the table next to the salt shaker in the shape of a plump old lady. "What's that?" she asked.

"Never mind," he said. "We need to talk. Do you remember last year, when you said to me, 'Do you and Mom ever have fun anymore?' "

Rosie shifted in her chair and felt her stomach dip as if she were on a roller coaster, except she wasn't hurtling down a track at fifty miles an hour. She was sitting in a kitchen chair that her mother had painted with fruit across the back. She remembered, of course. Rosie said to her father, "No, I forget."

Mr. Goldglitt cleared his throat and said, "Well, your question gave me a lot to think about, Rosie. Did your mom and I ever have any fun together?"

She remembered that her father hadn't answered yes. He hadn't answered her at all.

"I realized that the answer was no," he said. "That I could not remember an instant of fun with her in a very long time."

"Oh," Rosie replied. Her skin felt clammy and her face got hot, and she felt as though she'd run around the track a hundred times.

"Your mother and I have talked about it, and we've decided to get a divorce. It has nothing to do with you or your brother. I mean, you and Jimmy didn't cause this to happen. We . . ." Mr. Goldglitt cleared his throat. "We fell out of love," he said. And then he added, "We can't seem to get it back."

"*Try,*" Rosie said loudly. "*Try,*" she repeated before letting loose with a torrent of tears that she wanted to collect in a cup and throw in her father's face.

"We've tried, honey," he said softly. "For years."

"NO YOU HAVEN'T!" she screamed in a voice that was so disrespectful that if her dad didn't think he deserved to be yelled at, he would have reprimanded her.

"I know you're upset." He held out his hand and, with trembling fingers, pushed the package toward her. "I bought this for you."

Rosie picked it up and ripped off the paper. It was a book with the word *DIARY* written across it in pink script. "What's this for?" she asked, in the contemptuous tone that her mother detested even more than her father.

"I thought it might help, writing your thoughts in a journal. I know you're upset, but it's for the best, honey. In the long run, it will be better for all of us." He waited for an answer.

Rosie made him wait a long time. At last, she asked him, "What do you do for a living, Dad?"

"You know what I do," he said cautiously. "I'm a psychologist."

"And what does a psychologist do, Dad? You help people with their problems, don't you?" Rosie pressed on ruthlessly.

Her father's "yes" was so low she could barely hear it.

"So how come you can't help yourself? How come you can't fix your own marriage, Dad? I don't understand."

Tears filled her father's eyes as he spoke. "Rosie, if I had been my own patient, I would have tried to make myself see that my marriage had ended years ago. That fixing it was hopeless."

Rosie was speechless. Finally, she said, "So this is my big present? A divorce diary?"

"If you want to call it that."

"I should write down all my emotions and feelings in this little book, right?"

"I guess that's the idea."

Rosie pushed the chair that her mother had painted away from the table and picked up the diary. Her father had a glimmer of hope in his eyes. Then she walked across the room and dropped the book into the garbage can.

That night, her mother fished it out, cleaned it off, and left it on the shelf next to Rosie's bed. Rosie was quite tempted to throw it out the window. But there was something about the clean white unfilled pages. They beckoned her, and she didn't have the heart.

Rosie's leg had gone numb from sitting on the floor spying on her mother, when her brother, Jimmy, burst through the front door. The adults jumped up from the couch as if they were kids caught smoking cigarettes, which gave Rosie the chance to escape upstairs.

In the privacy of her bedroom, she picked up the diary. With a permanent marker, she wrote the word *KISSING* in big bold letters above the word *DIARY*. Then Rosie wrote:

Saturday night

Today, I watched my mother kiss. I must admit, it skeeved me out. My mother seemed to like it, which must mean she likes Sam, who is not too good-looking and has less hair than my father does. It doesn't seem to matter, though.

I hope if I ever get to kiss Robbie Romano,

I won't think of Mom and Sam. That would make me want to hurl.

    I am yours sincerely,
    Rosie Goldglitt
    also known as Rosie Gold-gag-me

P.S. I have decided that brushing your teeth is a must before mouth-to-mouth communication.

2

Rosie Goldglitt, Bitter about Her Name

Rosie draped a piece of string across the top of her diary so that she would know if anyone tampered with it. What if her mother discovered that her only daughter had spied on her love life with her balding boyfriend? She would go ballistic. There were certain grownup speeches that were repeated over and over, as if a replay button had been pressed. "Mothers have rights as human beings" was one of Mrs. Goldglitt's favorites, and Rosie had no wish to hear it. The comment about Sam wouldn't please her mother either. Just a few days before, she had said to her daughter, "Isn't he handsome?" Rosie rolled her eyes, which was *not* a smart move, as her mother had heard on *The Oprah Winfrey Show* that it was a sign of contempt.

Rosie's brother, Jimmy, was another matter. She suspected that, at fifteen, he already had experience in the realm of kissing. If Jimmy read the diary, one thing was certain. He would make Rosie's life a misery. But her brother didn't have a history of snooping. Her mother did. Rosie twisted a rubber band around the diary, tucked the string underneath, and buried it deep in her pajama drawer.

At breakfast the next day, Rosie munched on cereal while her mother made coffee and toasted Jimmy a bagel. She mumbled out loud that she needed to vacuum. Rosie doubted she would, and wondered if she would be hearing her mother's housework speech—"Cleaning is useless, because the dirt comes back." It was fine by Rosie if she didn't have to spend Sunday morning scrubbing out the bathroom. Sarah Singer's mother was a fanatic neat freak, which meant that her friend had had to miss several trips to the mall for weekend chores.

"Sam made me laugh. He said that the living room reminded him of the Mojave Desert," said her mother, smiling. "You know, dust balls, tumbleweed. Isn't that funny?"

"Hilarious," said Rosie, faking a smile. "I guess Sam likes a clean house like Dad did," she added, watching her mother's face.

Mrs. Goldglitt took the bagel out of the toaster and threw it on the plate with unusual force. "Jimmy!" she called. "Your breakfast is ready." She buttered the bagel silently.

Rosie pretended to be fascinated by the cereal box. Sometimes, she realized, she could play her mother like a violin. She knew how to rile her, and she was doing it a lot lately.

Jimmy made his entrance, yawning noisily, and plunked himself next to her. Mrs. Goldglitt put the buttered bagel in front of him, and he mumbled thanks.

"You're so spoiled," Rosie said idly, tracing her finger on the back of the box along the safari trail to the pot of gold.

"She'd make you one, too," her brother replied, biting into the bagel and wiping his mouth with the back of his hand.

"Use a napkin," said his mother.

"Gross," said Rosie, savoring a spoonful of sugary cereal. Mrs. Goldglitt, a health-food nut, had relented when they were little by letting them eat junk-food cereal every third day.

Jimmy chewed noisily and swigged down some milk.

"You eat like a pig," complained Rosie.

"What are you so grouchy about?" said her mother. She poured coffee into her favorite yellow mug, which said *I love you, Mother* across the front.

"I hate my name." Rosie eyeballed the cup, aware that she wasn't feeling much love for her mother. The coffee looked tempting, steaming and milky.

"It's a fine name." Her mother started reading the newspaper.

"Can I try some coffee?"

Jimmy piped up. "I'm three years older, and I'm not allowed. Why should you be?"

"It will stunt your growth," said Mrs. Goldglitt. "No one's allowed."

"I'm too tall already!" Rosie complained. Then she added what she knew would annoy her mother for sure. "Summer's mother lets her drink coffee every morning."

"I couldn't care less what Summer's mother lets her do," her mother said icily. "And what do you mean, you're too tall? You're too tall for what?"

"For Robbie," Rosie blurted out, instantly sorry. "I'm two inches taller than Robbie Romano."

"Two inches is nothing." Mrs. Goldglitt was dismissive. "In a few years, the boys will catch up to the girls."

"Hey, basketball is a good sport for giraffe girls," Jimmy teased her.

Rosie was annoyed. "Jimmy and I didn't buy you that *I love you* mug," she said.

"Hey!" said Jimmy. "Yes we did!"

Rosie ignored him. Why couldn't either of them understand how terrible it was being an oversized giant next to the cutest boy in the seventh grade? She needled her mother some more. "The baby-sitter bought it for us last year on Mother's Day. You were all upset by the divorce and everything, and she asked us what we were giving you, and Dad was gone, and we told her nothing. So she ran out and got this mug for you with her own money."

"We didn't have any," said Jimmy, scanning his mother's face.

Mrs. Goldglitt cupped the mug in her hands. "Hey, I loved it then, and I love it now. Nothing can change that."

Rosie couldn't seem to help herself and said, "Well, don't believe everything you read."

Her mother laughed. "You mean you don't love

me, like the mug says, because I won't let you drink coffee?"

"No, because I hate my name. Rosie Goldglitt is the worst name in the whole seventh-grade class," said Rosie. "Michael Kapp says it sounds like I'm an eighty-year-old lady. Couldn't we shorten it to Gold or something?"

Her mother raised an eyebrow. "First of all," she said, "Kapp was probably short for Kapowitz. And it's your heritage."

"It's Dad's heritage," Rosie muttered.

"Yes, Goldglitt is your father's last name, but it used to be Goldglitzen! And we named you Rosie after Grandma Rebecca. My mother was a beautiful lady, who gave birth to me, who gave birth to *you*! Some things can't change, you know, Rosie."

Rosie battled on. "Grandma Rebecca blew her nose on her scarf when we took her out."

Her mother laughed again. "She didn't realize. She thought it was her handkerchief."

"I almost barfed up my pancakes!" Rosie declared.

"Would you stop? I'm eating!" Jimmy yelled.

"Don't you remember, Jimmy?" Rosie continued, happy that her brother had joined the ranks of the grouchy. "We went to the nursing home to see Grandma Rebecca before she died. You, me, and Grandpa Joe took turns wheeling Grandma Rebecca down the street to the diner. Grandma ordered buckwheat pancakes, and while we were waiting—"

"Her nose started running, and she blew it on her scarf. Are you happy now that you've ruined my breakfast?" Jimmy said, tossing his bagel on the plate.

"Then she made the waitress pack up everyone's leftovers, and Grandma gave the soggy chewed-up half-eaten pancakes to her friends," said Rosie.

Jimmy couldn't help it and started laughing.

Their mother joined in. "I haven't ordered pancakes since!"

"Me either," said Rosie, mildly happy when Jimmy said, "Jimmy Goldglitt is the worst name in the tenth grade, too, you know."

But by then Mrs. Goldglitt had turned on the vacuum cleaner, and Rosie cleared her dishes and escaped the kitchen before her mother could find any chores for her to do.

The next morning wasn't much better for Rosie. Her mother was driving them to school wearing the same sparkly pink T-shirt that her best friend,

Lauren, owned. It was one thing having a cool mother. But would *any* twelve-year-old girl want her mother dressing like her? Rosie doubted it. Just the other day, Rosie had to stop her from buying a jar of body glitter at the pharmacy. Rosie shuddered at the thought that Sam would like it. A middle-aged mother should be dressing her age, not teetering down the aisle of the supermarket wearing high-heeled boots with pointy toes. Mrs. Goldglitt worked part-time as a receptionist at a local hair salon. She often told Rosie that it was fun playing "dress-up," which meant younger styles and higher heels and, sometimes, an embarrassed daughter.

"Other mothers wear sneakers," Rosie told her often.

"Sneakers are for the gym," her mother always replied.

Rosie's mother never left home without putting on lipstick. She carefully applied it in the car mirror before driving them to school that morning. Jimmy complained, "The crossing guard isn't going to care if you're wearing lipstick or not."

"I care," said his mother, blotting her lips on a tissue.

Rosie sniffed the air. "What am I smelling?"

"Jimmy, are you wearing cologne, honey?" said Mrs. Goldglitt.

Jimmy didn't answer, which made Rosie smile. She suspected that her brother had a crush of his own! Rosie had seen him hanging around Linda Reeves at the ice cream shop, looking kind of awkward. "Is Linda in your math class?" she asked him sweetly.

"None of your business," Jimmy replied.

"Be nice," said Mrs. Goldglitt, pulling out of the driveway with a lurch.

Homeroom started badly with a substitute teacher, who crucified the names as she read the attendance sheet. "Rosie Goldglatt, is that it? Or is it Goldglitt, or maybe Goldgitt?"

Tony Baskin said, "Goldtwit," which made a bunch of his friends laugh. Mary Katz joined them, warbling like a bird, saying, "Goldtwitter, Goldtwitter." Lauren agreed later that it wasn't the least bit funny.

Rosie looked daggers at the girl, a wasted gesture, as she couldn't catch her eye. She hated Mary Katz with every cell in her body. She hated her straight blond hair with its streaky highlights and her turned-up nose and her millionaire clothes. She hated her high-pitched laugh, which most people said was cute. She hated that Mary's mother let her wear black kohl eyeliner. But what Rosie hated most of all was that Mary Katz seemed to hate her back.

In English, Rosie signed her name on a quiz with a cute little rose at the end of it. Dressing up *Goldglitt* made her feel a little better. Lauren had given her a gold jelly pen that jazzed up the page when she signed her name, but it couldn't disguise the ugliness.

Why couldn't her parents have given her one of the popular names, like Jennifer or Jessica or Megan, for heaven's sake? Didn't parents know that they were building a personality when they named a baby? Rosie sighed, only half listening to the teacher babble on about Greek myths. What on earth were the Hoods thinking when they named their daughter Robin? That she would steal from the rich and give to the poor? How dumb was that, saddling their baby with a joke? Lauren's parents were brilliant. They gave their baby a popular name, which was just how Lauren turned out. Everybody liked her, even if she wasn't part of the inner circle. Rosie couldn't imagine what her own parents were thinking. Rosie Goldglitt, ninety-year-old spinster?

By the end of the day, Rosie started feeling better. She met Lauren by her locker, and neither of them had much homework. They walked home slowly in the afternoon sunshine, wondering whose house to visit. Lauren's house had tons of junk food, but Rosie's house had a new computer game. After some debate, Cheez Doodles won.

They were rounding the corner in Lauren's direction when they heard a noise coming from the enormous rosebush at the far end of the school grounds.

"What's that?" Rosie whispered, stopping to listen. Lauren joined her, and when the large shrub shivered and shook, the girls jumped back.

"What are we doing?" Rosie hissed. "It could be a crazy person with a knife or something!"

A branch snapped and a hand emerged from the bottom. Rosie and Lauren screamed so loudly that the hand coming from the bush disappeared. They heard a screech that didn't belong to a girl.

A boy jumped out, wide-eyed as if he'd seen a ghost, holding on to a tennis ball for dear life. "What's the matter?" he yelled, looking around for what he must have thought was a murderer at least. At the sight of the girls, he took one step back, catching his foot on the root of the tree behind him. Robbie Romano, Rosie's biggest crush ever, fell over backward.

"We heard you in the bushes and it scared us," said Lauren, holding out a hand, which Robbie didn't take. Rosie was envious. Her friend could actually talk to Robbie without stumbling on her words.

He scrambled to his feet and said, "I was looking for my tennis ball, and I heard you guys screaming! I ripped my hand off in that thorny rosebush!"

"Are you okay?" Rosie stammered. "We're sorry we scared you!"

"Scared me?" His voice was shrill. "Don't make me laugh! I should have known it was you! Rosie Gold*twit*! Or is it Rosie *half-wit*?" He practically spat out the names and walked away, shaking his head.

There went the day. The Cheez Doodles didn't help Rosie's mood at all. They left a cheesy taste in her mouth, which added to her feeling of dread. She left Lauren's house early and walked home quickly, up the stairs, and into her bedroom, where she shut the door.

Rosie opened up her pajama drawer and took out her diary, removing the string and the rubber band. Then she wrote:

Monday afternoon

Today was one of the worst days of my life. I finally got to talk to Robbie Romano, and I embarrassed him by saying I was sorry we scared him. What was I thinking? Then he called me Rosie Goldtwit AND Rosie Half-wit, and left me standing there feeling stupid. Lauren says that he'll forget all about it soon. I know he won't. My life is ruined. I'm signing this with sorrow,

Rosie Goldglitt, Twit of the Century

P.S. I snuck some coffee before school this morning, and when I was pouring it out in the sink, my mother came in, but she didn't say anything.
P.P.S. I hate hate hate my name.
P.P.P.S. Coffee smells so good and tastes so bad.

3

Rosie Goldglitt Is So Mad She'd Like to Goldspit

Rosie thought it was odd how the day after disaster struck, nothing had changed. She ate her usual bowl of cereal, cornflakes this time instead of Lucky Charms, and read the back of the box at the kitchen table. Jimmy managed to make her grouchier by pointing out a blemish on her chin. He should talk, with five pimples on his forehead to her one. As usual, the two of them sat in the car waiting for their mother to put on her lipstick. Jimmy grumbled, and Mrs. Goldglitt told him that daylight was best for applying makeup. Jimmy replied that the supermarket checkout girl would not drop dead if she wasn't wearing lipstick. His mother told him not to be fresh. She pulled up to the school as he was laughing derisively, and he let himself out of the car. Rosie followed, straight into

Robbie, who turned his back so quickly that she felt a gust of air. How could Rosie's life possibly be the same when her heart was broken?

Shortly after school ended, she was back at Lauren's with her friends, eating vanilla wafers and drinking regular milk, which tasted like a milk shake compared to her mother's skim. Rosie was utterly miserable. The day had gone from bad to worse. Robbie was no longer ignoring her. In order to be ignored, you had to be alive, didn't you? Rosie was less than a speck on the planet. As far as Robbie was concerned, she didn't exist.

Sarah Singer and Summer Adams sat on the couch, urging Rosie to give them all the details.

"Is it true he fell over backward?" Summer asked.

"He took one look at her and fell head over heels," said Sarah, clasping her hands to her chest.

"Head over heels in hate," said Rosie glumly. "He called me Goldtwit and Half-wit."

"Nasty!" said Sarah. "And he rhymed!"

"Maybe you should try liking Eli," suggested Summer. "Didn't you have a crush on him in the fifth grade?"

"Not anymore," Rosie answered, wondering why Lauren wasn't saying a word.

"Picture him gone," said Sarah. "My mom had a patient who wanted to go on a diet, and she hypnotized him into believing that cockroaches were crawling on his chocolate ice cream. He lost thirty pounds. Hey, I know what! Picture liquid Drano poured on your heart when you think about Robbie!"

"My heart's not a toilet!" Rosie protested. How perfect for Sarah to suggest a cleaning product, with a neat-freak psychiatrist for a mother.

Summer said in a worried voice, "Wouldn't Drano kill her?" Everyone but Rosie burst out laughing.

"My mother won't even let me try coffee," said Rosie, "so Drano's out!" Lighten up, she said to herself, but happiness was hard to fake. She looked over at Lauren, sitting quietly on a pillow. "What do you think I should do?" she asked.

Lauren hesitated. Then she took a deep breath and said, "I don't think picturing Drano will work. But best friends speak the truth, and I have to say it. Forget about Robbie."

Tears sprang to Rosie's eyes, and Sarah, the only twelve-year-old who carried tissues with her, gave Rosie one.

"I know you like him." Lauren grabbed Rosie's

hand. "But if you had spinach in your teeth, I'd tell you. He was mean all day, and you really didn't do anything wrong, did you?"

"No," said Rosie, wiping her eyes.

"But Rosie doesn't like spinach, do you, Rosie?" said Summer, desperate to cheer her up. "She hates anything green."

"Speaking of green," said Sarah, "Mary Katz ordered this gross-smelling green dish at Sal's the other day."

"Nasty," said Summer. "Just like her." Summer didn't like Mary any more than Rosie did. Mary had called her *dumb* in the third grade, which had morphed into *Dumb and Dumber Summer* for the whole year.

"It was broccoli rabe, and it smelled disgusting," said Sarah.

"If we're going to forget about anyone," said Summer, "let's forget about Mary. Besides, Rosie, you eat green! You ate lime Jell-O at my house the other day!"

"Robbie eats Jell-O every day," said Rosie. So much for forgetting about Robbie Romano.

"My sister says, sometimes if you ignore the boy, he'll come back," said Lauren forgivingly.

"Like a boomerang," said Summer, which was

no help at all, as Rosie envisioned Robbie whizzing through the air and knocking her over.

"He can't come back. I never had him in the first place," Rosie said.

"Like in *The Wizard of Oz*!" said Summer. "Dorothy says, 'If I ever go looking for my heart's desire again, I won't look any further than my own backyard, because if it isn't there, I never really lost it to begin with!' I love that show!" Summer wrinkled up her forehead. "Then again," she said, "Robbie hasn't ever been in your backyard, has he?"

"He used to say hello and goodbye, which was way better than being hated!" Rosie reached for her eleventh vanilla wafer.

"Ask your brother what he thinks," said Lauren. "He's a boy. While you're at it, find out if I should ask Tommy Stone to the dance."

"Talk to Jimmy?" said Rosie doubtfully. Certainly she could ask him about Tommy Stone. Lauren's crush was Robbie's opposite. Perhaps that was why she and Lauren got along. Lauren liked boys who were outgoing and funny, although Rosie secretly thought that they were noisy show-offs. Take Tommy, for instance. When he walked into the cafeteria, you knew he had arrived. He made barfing noises standing over the sloppy joes until somebody laughed, usually one of the boys in his little trio, either Tony Baskin or Eddie Duval. Or he'd take Eddie's baseball cap, jam it on Tony's head, and say, "Much better! A fashion plus." If someone dropped a plate and it landed with a clatter, Tommy was the first one to hoot and holler until everyone joined in. Rosie couldn't see herself liking a hooter or a hollerer. She liked the quieter boys who surprised her with their funniness. The ones who didn't try so hard to be noticed.

Rosie reached for the cookie box and ate her twelfth vanilla wafer. She closed the box. Thirteen cookies would be a mistake. She had had enough bad luck.

Lauren changed the subject. "Can you believe Mrs. Geller is ruining the weekend with a project?"

Sarah sighed. "Build a castle. It sounds so messy. My mother's going to freak. Why can't we just draw one?"

"I'm going to build mine out of sugar cubes," said Summer.

"I'm going to write a letter of protest," Rosie said, shaking her head. Just a few hours before, in history class, the teacher had given them an assignment to build a medieval castle and label its parts. History wasn't Rosie's favorite subject, but she sat next to Robbie, so it was the highlight of the day. He mumbled so low that she could barely hear him, "She's got one color missing in that Crayola box called a brain." Rosie laughed so loudly that everyone looked. Everyone but Robbie, who cast his eyes at the ceiling, examined the floor, doodled in his notebook, or stared straight ahead. When Rosie bumped into him later in the hallway, his blank stare was so chilling that she didn't exist.

"Mrs. Geller ruined the weekend all right," said Rosie, thinking that more than her weekend had been ruined.

The rest of the week wasn't much better. Robbie continued ignoring Rosie. Rosie continued to mope. She never even bothered telling her mother about the history project due Monday morning. On Saturday, Rosie informed her that she needed art supplies to build a castle and label its parts.

Mrs. Goldglitt fumed. "Now you're telling me? How the heck do we build a castle? With clay? Popsicle sticks? Papier-mâché? I'm not an architect, for heaven's sake."

"I'm going to be doing it," Rosie said. " 'Be inventive,' " she read off the assignment sheet. " 'Use any material you like.' " Was it her fault she couldn't drive a car to the art store? Was it her fault that Mrs. Geller didn't give a flying fig about ruining her weekend?

"You're going to do it? With what?" said her mother, instructing Rosie to wipe off the table and make the labels while she went to the art store. Then she stormed out of the house, returning an hour later with poster board, cardboard, oaktag, cans of spray paint, a matt knife, and a sealed bag of clay that was supposed to harden when it dried.

Rosie propped a picture of a medieval castle against a vase of dried flowers and began rolling strips of clay to make the base of the castle. Placing a piece of poster board on a magazine, Rosie drew a line marking the edge of the first wall, and picked up the matt knife.

"You'll cut your finger off," her mother barked, grabbing the knife out of her daughter's hand. Mumbling to herself, she began cutting, but the knife veered off to the side. With more huffing and puffing than Rosie thought was necessary, her mother rummaged through a drawer in the desk in the living room and found a wooden ruler. Her face was getting redder by the minute, and when the matt knife caught against the edge of the ruler, Rosie thought her mother would have a stroke.

"This is how I get to spend my day off?" shouted her mother, running downstairs to the basement and yelling upstairs, "Call your father and ask him if he took the metal ruler! I'm not buying another one!"

"Mom, take it *easy*!" Rosie called to her, but before she could dial, her mother was upstairs, grabbing the phone from her. She punched in the numbers and said, "Bob? I need the metal ruler to help your daughter with her damned project." Then she said, "I'm not swearing, I just need the damned ruler," followed by, "Please, Bob, no lectures, I'm at the end of my rope." There was a silence, and Rosie's mother turned to her and said grimly, "Go downstairs and look in Dad's workroom and it should be in the drawer with the missing handle."

She muttered thank you into the receiver, and Rosie found the ruler, and work resumed. Her mother managed to cut a straight line without lopping off her finger, and they anchored the pieces of card in the clay. Then Rosie unrolled a roll of paper towels so that they could use the cardboard tube for the turret.

"Isn't it too small?" said Rosie, risking another explosion from her mother.

Mrs. Goldglitt took one look and threw it in the trash can, while Rosie rolled a piece of oaktag into a cylinder, taping it together.

"Good," said her mother grudgingly.

By this time, Mrs. Goldglitt's lips had formed a permanent frown as she fashioned another piece of oaktag into a cone that the two of them taped to the top of the tower. Rosie carried the castle carefully outside and went back for the cans of spray paint.

"I'm having a cup of coffee," said her mother. "You're on your own."

Rosie painted the water a pretty shade of blue. The sun was shining, there was a gentle breeze blowing, and she was nearly done. A cardinal flew by, and Rosie smiled at the flash of red. She had the rest of the weekend to have fun with her friends. They'd go bowling soon, and have lunch at Sal's, maybe browse next door at the pharmacy. Life wasn't so bad. Why let someone like Robbie Romano ruin her day?

Rosie took the cap off the final can and began spraying silver paint on the castle walls. The wind picked up and sent the spray traveling in the opposite direction. Rosie looked down at her favorite pair of jeans. They were speckled with color. She started screaming just about the time that Tommy and Eddie and Tony were passing by. Tommy the Hooter began laughing hysterically, pointing at Rosie. The two boys joined him, marionette puppets following their leader in his stupid dance.

Mrs. Goldglitt opened the door, wearing the daisy top that Lauren had worn to school the day before. She glared at the boys, her arms crossed as if she were Rosie's prison guard. Was it the look on her face or the skimpy top on a grown older woman that scared the boys away? Rosie would never know the truth, because she would never ask the question, never, never, never, in a million years.

On Sunday morning, Rosie walked into the dining room, where the castle sat drying on pieces of newspaper. She screamed for the second time that weekend, a bloodcurdling noise that brought her mother and Jimmy racing down the stairs in their pajamas. Mrs. Goldglitt stared at the wrecked castle. The clay had dried, but the walls had collapsed and fallen over. To Rosie's horror, a tear trickled down her mother's cheek.

Mrs. Goldglitt ran upstairs, threw on her tightest jeans and her high-heeled boots, and said, "Come with me," between clenched teeth. They drove to Home Depot, and Mrs. Goldglitt walked briskly up and down the aisles until she found a man wearing a Home Depot badge. Then she proceeded to bore him with the castle saga, except that Rosie knew he wasn't bored, by the way he stared at her mother's animated face. Something was happening, the lipstick, the makeup, the sparkle in her mother's eyes. He was jumping through hoops now, and would have built a house out of bricks and mortar for her if he'd been asked. Rosie heard the man say, "Call if you need me, my name is Tim!" Mrs. Goldglitt's laugh floated across the nails and ratchets as she walked away saying, "Thank you so much, Tim, but we'll be fine."

Rosie's mother was cheerful in the car, but as they approached the house, she grumbled out loud, "This project of yours cost me a hundred bucks! I have half a mind to write your teacher a letter! Gas, art supplies, your jeans, what else?"

"Your bad mood," said Rosie, looking sideways at her mother, who started to laugh. Thank goodness for Tim, Rosie thought, but she didn't dare say it.

Rosie used electrical tape, Big Shot Mr. Fix-It Tim's idea, to fix the walls. It looked downright tacky, but she didn't care. The weekend had finished with a nasty bang. She went upstairs and wrote in her diary:

Sunday night

If I had the nerve to write to Mrs. Geller, this is what I'd say:

Dear Mrs. Geller,
Thanks so much for ruining my weekend and for making my mother go nuts and broke with your stupid project. It certainly was appreciated.

Sincerely yours,
Rosie Goldglitt / otherwise known as
Rosie Gold-pissed-off / also known as
Rosie Gold-bitter that the weekend was ruined

P.S. I wonder what Robbie did for his project? Most of all, I wonder if he'll hate me on Monday morning.

4

Rosie
Makes a Decision

Rosie's mother apologized at the dinner table on Monday.

"For what?" said Jimmy, eating forkfuls of macaroni and cheese as if he hadn't eaten for three days.

"Let her speak," said Rosie, deciding in an instant that her mother should explain her horrible behavior.

"For acting like a nut all weekend, Rosie. I was terrible." Mrs. Goldglitt toyed with her salad. "It was . . . stressful."

"Oh," said Rosie, thinking that it wasn't much of an explanation.

Her mother continued. "Sam didn't call when he said he would, and by Saturday I hadn't heard from him, and . . . I was upset and I took it out on you." She sighed.

"It's scary, Mom."

"You're scary," said Jimmy. "Is there any more mac and cheese?"

Mrs. Goldglitt jumped up, despite Rosie's telling him to get it himself. "What's scary?"

"You sound like me," said Rosie, forming an *R* for Robbie with the remainder of the noodles on her plate.

"I'm back in the dating game," said her mother. "Which means I'm back in high school all over again."

Rosie took her fork and wrecked the letter she'd formed. What was she thinking, anyway? "I've been upset the whole week because someone won't talk to me."

Her mother was a good listener when she wasn't feeling stressed. "Who?" she said, giving Rosie her undivided attention.

"Remember that guy Robbie I told you about? The one I'm taller than?"

Her mother nodded.

Rosie told her the story about scaring Robbie in the bushes.

"He screamed?" said Jimmy, smirking. He coughed, saying "Loser" under his breath.

"Look who's talking! You screamed at the last scary movie we saw, and couldn't go to sleep without the lights on for days!" It was sad how she couldn't stop herself from defending Robbie.

"That was years ago," said Jimmy, digging into the second helping on his plate.

Rosie continued. "We scared him to death, and he fell over backward, and all I said was, 'We're sorry we frightened you,' and he got furious at me and hasn't talked to me since."

"I see," said her mother, pursing her lips.

"You see what?"

"She sees that he's a baby for screaming, and she sees that he's a clumsy geek for falling over." Jimmy stood up and uttered a high-pitched sound, falling over backward onto the kitchen floor.

"Ignore him," said Mrs. Goldglitt, trying hard not to smile. "Jimmy, get off the floor. It hasn't been washed in a year."

Rosie waited while her mother took a container out of the freezer. "Does anyone want some?" she said, scooping some mocha chip ice cream into a bowl. "I haven't learned much," she said, "but here's what I know. Never ask a man if you've

40

scared him, Rosie. Particularly if he's a caveman type, or under the age of twenty-one. He'll think you're calling him a wimp."

"That's it?" said Rosie, exasperated. "I was afraid he'd hurt himself, falling over like that, and he thinks I'm calling him a wimp?"

"It's that male mentality," said Mrs. Goldglitt, reading the back of the container. "One hundred fifty calories for half a cup? That's one spoonful, isn't it?" She shoved the ice cream back into the freezer and took out the chocolate syrup.

"Why does it matter if he's under twenty-one?" said Rosie.

"He's young," said her mother, squirting syrup on her dish of ice cream so that it made a terrible sound.

Jimmy started hooting and slapping his thigh.

"See what I mean?" said their mother, laughing. "They're young and immature, and their self-esteem is shaky. Boys that age are so full of pride that you can't insult their manhood. And he might take after his father," she added, "who I happen to know is a Neanderthal."

"How do you know?" said Rosie curiously. "You met his father?"

"Years ago," said her mother. She changed the

subject abruptly. "Make me work out after I eat this ice cream."

"Can I have some?" said Jimmy. "It might help my low self-esteem."

"It will help you even more if you get it your-self," said his mother. "Anyway, you were in kin-dergarten, and it was the first day of school, and I'm parked there and watching to make sure that you get inside safely, and he clips my fender when he's backing up!"

"What did you do?" said Rosie.

Her mother snorted. "I got out of the car to look, and he yells, 'What do you think you were doin'?' Can you imagine? *He* cracks into my car, and says, 'What do you think you were doin'?' The nerve!"

Rosie watched her mother get annoyed all over again. Then her mother took a spoonful of ice cream and got sugar-rush happier.

"This is delicious," she said. "So I tell him, 'I'm waiting to make sure that my little girl gets into school, do you have a problem with that?' He says, 'I have a problem with you parking so close to my van that I can't get out!' And he gets into his van and drives off! Can you imagine? He leaves me there with a dented fender, and I go ask the crossing guard, 'Who *is* that jerk?' And she says, 'That's little Robbie Romano's father, Al.' "

Rosie rested her head on the kitchen table.

Her mother said in a soft voice, "Remember that boys of twelve are unable to process their feelings yet. They're *way* behind girls, Rosie."

"Maybe he remembered that you insulted his father," Rosie mumbled from the table edge.

"I doubt it. Calling you names might mean that he likes you. He was embarrassed and confused, so he just lashed out."

"Or he hates you," said Jimmy, scooping ice cream into a dish.

"Like I hate you," said Rosie.

"Please. No hating in my kitchen," said their mother. "Jimmy, try not to live up to the immaturity I'm talking about."

Rosie said, "He ignored me last week. He ignored me today. I hate to say it, but I think Jimmy is right."

"Mark my words," said her mother. "It might mean just the opposite."

Rosie couldn't help it. She lifted up her head from the table and rolled her eyes at her mother, who hadn't seen Robbie's face when he'd called her Rosie Goldtwit. How could she forget the look he'd given her today, when she just couldn't help herself and blurted out, "Are you still mad at me?" It was straight from one of those shows where the contestant has to drink a concoction of worms, slugs, and cow's intestines. Rosie had made him sick to his stomach.

Later, watching television, Jimmy surprised her by saying, "Mom could be right, you know. He might like you."

"Really?" said Rosie, pressing him to go further, but her brother clammed up.

Rosie asked him, "Do you think Lauren should ask Tommy Stone to the dance? She wants to know."

"Hey, if he likes her, it will turn out fine. If he doesn't, it's not a good idea."

"Great," said Rosie. "She'll be happy to hear."

Jimmy laughed. "Hey, what do you want from me? Didn't Mom tell you that girls are way more evolved than boys?"

Mrs. Goldglitt entered the living room wearing sweats and sneakers. She hopped onto the elliptical trainer that their father had bought her before the divorce. Pressing some buttons, she asked Rosie to turn up the television.

Rosie climbed off the couch and adjusted the

sound. "How come I always have to do every-thing? Why can't you ask Jimmy?"

"Jeez," said her mother. "That must be my Neanderthal-woman side. The woman cooks and she cleans and she tends to the children. And the man goes out to hunt and provide for the family, you know? I'll try to improve."

"Women move faster," said Jimmy, slouching happily on the couch.

They watched television to the monotonous sound of their mother walking on metal pedals.

At the commercial, Rosie said, "Hey, Mom, so what put you in a better mood anyway?"

Mrs. Goldglitt walked faster to the tune of the commercial. "He called," she said simply.

Right before bed, Rosie wrote in her diary:

Monday night

Dear Diary,

My mother was a basket case all weekend because her boyfriend didn't call. I guess I take after her, because I was a wreck all week, wondering how to get Robbie to talk to me. I can't believe she had this fight with Robbie Romano's father. That's just great. We'll go out, and he'll realize that he likes me a lot, and I'll meet his father, and he'll say, Your mother is nuts, and Robbie will say, Like mother, like daughter, and he'll never see me again.

This is all wishful thinking, of course, because as of today, he still hasn't spoken a word to me. Like Summer says, it's hard to get back what you never really had in the first place. I definitely want to decrushify. He's a lost cause.

I give up, I really do. I'll try not to mention his name anymore.

Yours truly,
Rosie ~~Gold~~-~~Quit~~

5

It's All Greek to Rosie, Including Boys

$\mathcal{M}$r. Woo made it hard for Rosie to decrushify. English was Rosie's favorite subject because the teacher, Mr. Woo, managed to keep it interesting, having them act out passages from books they were reading and giving them assignments that didn't bore them to death. Getting an A in English was easy for Rosie. Getting a B– in math was much harder.

The halls were crowded on the way to class. Rosie's jean jacket accidentally brushed against Robbie, who jammed his back so hard against the locker that the imprint of the lock might have embossed his skin. Avoiding Rosie had been taken one step further. Rosie was a germ, and she half expected him to get out a packet of antiseptic wipes to kill any lingering Goldglitt bacteria. Being a germ was totally exhausting, and Rosie came to the conclusion that it sucked.

Rosie settled in her seat, with Summer behind her, next to Robbie, and Lauren to her right. Although she couldn't see Robbie, just his presence made her jittery. Was he staring at the back of her head with contempt? She would have to ask Summer. Did he make fun of her when she raised her hand? Ordinarily she would turn and talk to Summer so that she could catch a glimpse of him. Poor Summer would have to be ignored, or lean forward and talk in Rosie's ear if she had something to say. Rosie would not budge in her seat. She would not turn around.

Rosie opened up her English notebook. Inside the cover she had drawn a heart with two sets of initials inside: *RR* and *RG*. Rosie took her pen and colored in the letters. Then she drew bold lines one way and the other, over and over, until she could barely distinguish the letters beneath. She drew an X across the network of scribbles for good measure. Her mother was wrong and Lauren was right. The negative attention didn't mean that he liked her. It meant that he didn't. From this moment forward, Robbie Romano didn't exist.

What was it Grandma Rebecca liked to say?

Man made plans and God laughed. Except that in this case, Rosie made the plan to decrushify and Mr. Woo laughed by announcing a project on Greek mythology. Each group would be assigned a god or a goddess, and they would present their myth in front of the class. There was a chorus of groans. For a split second, Rosie wished she were next to Robbie, so that she could hear his perfect put-down. Didn't Mr. Woo ever have lunch with Mrs. Geller? Didn't he know that they had just recovered from a history project that had ruined their weekend and cost her mother a hundred dollars? And that Rosie's castle wasn't half as good as Summer's, made entirely of sugar cubes? And that Sarah's castle was the best in the class, with her father, the architect, helping her? Couldn't Mr. Woo give them all a break?

"Be original!" Mr. Woo said cheerfully, as though he'd just announced a pizza party for the next day. To Rosie's relief, he called out first names only, but her heart did a flip-flop as *Rosie* and *Robbie* and *Mary* and *Teresa* reverberated in the air. It was a plot against her, it had to be. Rosie cast a glance at Lauren, who raised an eyebrow as if to say, "This should be interesting."

Being in a group with Robbie was bad enough,

but Mary Katz was worse. As for Teresa Tubby, what could be said about a girl who lived in a world of her own? How could she not, with a name like that? If Rosie's body was shaped like a pear, skinny on top and rounder at the bottom, and Lauren's body was teen-model shapely, Teresa's body was straight and boxy, with no curves about it. It was her father's fault. She had grown into the name that she'd inherited, and maybe, just maybe, it was worse than Goldglitt.

Rosie wondered if having a name like Tubby made you strong at birth. It was kind of amazing how Teresa didn't care what anyone thought. Did she get up in the morning and ask herself, "How bizarre can I look today?" Designer clothes had no place in Teresa's wardrobe. On an ordinary day, she might put on a pair of fuchsia pink pants and a red plaid shirt (not retro, but straight out of her mother's time-warped closet), with a hundred buttons pinned on a man's green vest—peace signs from the sixties, weird rock bands that nobody had ever heard of, candy logos, Bart Simpson, Donald Duck. She wore her hair in bunches, with pompoms and different-colored ribbons. People stared at her as she walked down the street; children turned and pointed. A dangling key chain hooked to her jeans had so many jingling keys and coins and characters on it that dogs barked when they heard her coming. Secretly, Rosie admired her. Teresa didn't care what people thought of her. Rosie did. Way too much.

The groups formed huddles, and noisy discussion began. Mary Katz found her way to the back of the room, pulling a desk close to Robbie's. He didn't move away. Rosie focused on Teresa Tubby as if she were the most fascinating person in the world. She despised Mary, snuggling up to Robbie. She couldn't look at either of them.

Mary Katz stood up for the world to see her tight pink T-shirt with *PRINCESS* written across it in purple rhinestones. She stood behind Robbie, leaning over him so that her flaxen hair draped across the top of his head.

"Is Rapunzel a myth?" Rosie heard Robbie ask her. "Is this rehearsal?"

"Huh?" said Mary, planting her chin on him.

"You know," he said, touching the blond hair that hung past his ears. "The story about the girl who gets put in a tower, and her boyfriend prince says, 'Rapunzel, Rapunzel, let down your golden hair'?"

Mary's laugh was bell-like. "That's a fairy tale,

silly. I wanted to see what you looked like as a blond!"

He was laughing now, not calling her names. What was it Rosie's mother had called his father? Neanderthal. Like father, like son.

To Rosie's relief, Mr. Woo arrived, and Mary sat down at her desk again. He gave them their assignment: Demeter, Persephone, and Hades.

Robbie protested. "Hey, Mr. Woo! How come you gave us three myths?" Teresa corrected him, reciting the myth behind the names, and Mr. Woo made her team captain. Mary scribbled her address on a piece of paper and gave it to Robbie. "We'll do it at my house," she announced.

"Mansion," said Teresa when she heard the address.

"Whatever," said Mary.

A couple of days later, when Mrs. Goldglitt drove Rosie to Mary's house, their eyes widened as they passed through the gate that said PRIVATE ROAD, down a long tree-lined street, and into her circular driveway. The edge of a tennis court could be seen in back, and two fancy silver cars were parked in front of a garage that looked big enough

to hold Rosie's house. She waved goodbye to her mother and rang the doorbell, half expecting a butler to appear.

Mary answered, decked out in what looked like brand-new clothes with the tags snipped off. Rosie recognized the same Juicy Couture T-shirt that her mother wouldn't buy her because it was too expensive, her exact words being, "Twenty dollars more for a handful of fake diamonds? I don't think so." Rosie followed Mary through three rooms that all looked like living rooms into another large space she called "the den." Robbie was already there.

"Hey," he said, aiming the word at wallpaper that Rosie's mother would die for.

"Hey," Rosie answered, and Mary disappeared when the doorbell chimed again.

"This house is amazing. They must be rich," said Rosie.

Robbie didn't answer, and Rosie made a mental note to borrow Lauren's dog muzzle for any future meetings.

Jangling noises signaled that Teresa had arrived. She breezed in and started pulling books out of her knapsack, talking nonstop. "I got three books about Demeter and Persephone out of the library.

One is a picture book, which makes it easier to write a play about them. Another name for Demeter is Ceres, you know. We get the word *cereal* from Ceres, because she's the goddess of the harvest." Teresa rummaged some more and pulled out a box of Lucky Charms with the name crossed out in Magic Marker. Above it, she had written LUCKY CERES.

Robbie looked blankly at the cereal box. Rosie saw him exchange dumb glances with Mary. It annoyed her. Had *they* gone to the library like Teresa had? Rosie had hastily pulled a few articles off the Internet, and that was it. Mary giggled, as if she was sharing a private joke with Robbie. Rosie resisted the urge to empty the Lucky Charms over Mary's perfect blond hair.

Teresa fanned them with a stack of typed pages and said, "Rosie, you can be the mother, Demeter, okay? Hey, we could call her De Mutter! Get it? Demeter? De mother? De Mutter? That's funny. Anyhow . . ." She reached into her bottomless Mary Poppins satchel and pulled out a gigantic fruit-patterned dress that resembled a beach bag. "This would be a good costume for you, wouldn't it? Goddess of the Harvest?"

"Who am I?" said Mary, eager for her assignment.

"You're Rosie's beautiful daughter, Persephone," said Teresa, very pleased with her casting.

Rosie held the dress in her hand. Not only did she have a *body* shaped like a pear, but she'd be wearing a dress covered with strawberries and bananas and peaches and plums that was bigger and uglier than any of Grandma Rebecca's nightgowns. And she'd be playing Mary's mother.

Teresa continued. "Persephone was raised among flowers and she looked like one, too, so you fit the part."

More like the Venus flytrap, thought Rosie, watching Mary purr next to Robbie. She glared at Teresa, who took no notice, saying, "And that leaves Robbie. Robbie, you can be Hades."

Robbie plopped down on the couch and said, "What's his thing?"

"He's the God of the Dead."

Robbie collapsed in a heap and said, "Then I don't have do anything, do I?" He closed his eyes and lolled his tongue out of his mouth.

Rosie couldn't help laughing along with Mary.

Teresa looked mildly annoyed and said, "Guys,

do you even know the story here? It's why we have the division of the seasons. Winter and summer and spring and fall?"

"If we moved to Florida, where they don't have any seasons, we wouldn't have to do this anymore!" said Robbie, no longer dead.

Mary's laughter outdid Rosie's, and Teresa shushed her. "Persephone, you're out painting and you see this bush that you don't want to put in the picture. So you pull it out, and the hole gets bigger, and out leap six black horses and a golden chariot with you in it, Robbie. And you take her away."

"That's called kidnapping, isn't it?" said Robbie. "Can they put gods in jail?"

"My uncle owns horses," said Mary.

Rosie resisted calling her an idiot. "I don't think we can bring a horse into school," she said sweetly.

"A chariot would be tough," added Robbie, appearing to side with Rosie, which cheered her immensely.

Teresa ignored them. "Robbie, you take her to your underground kingdom."

"A lot of action for the God of the Dead," he answered. Rosie tried not to laugh, she really did. Why should she make him think he was funny when he had been so mean?

56

Teresa continued. "You try to make her love you, Robbie. You give her all sorts of presents. Rubies, diamonds."

"What, no Kate Spade pocketbook?" Mary asked.

"She plays jacks with the jewels," Teresa told her.

"Who's Kate Spade?" said Robbie.

"A great designer," said Mary.

"Of spades?" Robbie looked so dumbfounded that Rosie had to laugh.

"Of handbags," said Rosie, delighted by Robbie's lack of knowledge when it came to Mary's fashion name-dropping.

Teresa pulled a handful of junk jewelry out of her bag, the kind Grandma's sister, Aunt Sadie, liked to wear. "You can break these apart and use them, Mary. But, Hades, you have trouble winning her over. This girl is hard to please!"

"*Moi?*" said Mary, in the only French word Rosie knew.

"Yes, and, Demeter, *you* go crazy!" said Teresa, directing her attention to Rosie, who sat up straighter. "You're furious and heartbroken, and you want revenge! You mess up the world! You won't let crops grow. Your husband, that's Zeus, he goes along with it. I guess I'll play him, he's King of the Gods, but believe me, Zeus doesn't mess with his wife! Winds start blowing and crops aren't growing, hey, that rhymes, maybe we should write a song about it!"

"Or use sound effects," said Robbie, whistling like the wind.

"Not bad! Let's use it. I'll put it in the script." Teresa pulled an apple out of her trusty bag. "My mom wouldn't let me buy a pomegranate," she explained. "So we'll have to make believe. Mary, you eat six seeds from the pomegranate, which means marriage. You're stuck!"

"We can use M&M's," said Mary, looking pleased with herself.

Rehearsal continued, with Teresa typing the skit into Mary's computer, Robbie trying to be funny, Mary giggling, and Rosie unable to decrushify. She sat like a lump on Mary's plush floral couch, holding the costume that would soon make her look like a big fat bowl of fruit.

That night, she wrote in her diary:

Thursday night
Not much to report. Saw Robbie today and couldn't help laughing at his silly jokes. I think

I've turned into my mother, who laughs at everything that Sam says. I tried to ignore him, but Mary got me going, cooing next to him. I guess I'm stuck.

Signing off on my fruitless crush,
Rosie Gold-plum-pear-peach-pit-glitt!

6

Rosie Goldglitt's Skit

Zeus, Demeter, Hades, and Persephone fine-tuned their script as much as they could, printed up copies, and met that Sunday for a quick rehearsal. Robbie continued to address the wallpaper, but Teresa Tubby was such a taskmaster that there was very little time to take notice.

By Wednesday morning, Rosie was so nervous she could barely eat her bowl of unhealthy cereal. It was her group's turn to perform today, and not even Lucky Charms would go down.

Rosie's mother was all smiles, offering her daughter a variety of choices: waffles, toast, French toast sticks. Rosie looked at her suspiciously. "Why are you so happy, Mom?" she asked.

Her mother laughed and said, schoolgirl giggly, "Sam called me early this morning."

"We have an alarm clock," Jimmy said in between bagel bites.

"Be nice," said Mrs. Goldglitt, her smile undimmed.

It was unsettling. Wasn't Rosie supposed to be the one feeling giddy after a boy she liked showed her some attention? If her mother had never seemed happier, it felt like the opposite for Rosie.

"Break a leg," Mrs. Goldglitt told her as she got out of the car.

"Don't make a fool of yourself," Jimmy added, bounding ahead of her.

Would it kill her brother to be seen walking in with her? thought Rosie, nearly killing herself when her foot caught on the inside of her very flared jeans. A hand found her elbow and steadied her. She looked into the blue eyes of Billy Jones, who said, "Your mother didn't really mean you should break a leg, Rosie!"

"What can I say?" said Rosie, laughing. "I follow directions!" It was funny how easily she could talk to Billy, whose friendly smile forced her to overlook the whoosh of body odor that nearly knocked her out on a queasy stomach. Red-faced and sweaty, he must have run to school at break-

61

neck speed. His deodorant, if he used one, wasn't working.

"I'll see you in English," Billy threw over his shoulder. "I'm up first!"

Rosie resisted telling him to shower first. "Break a leg!" she yelled after him down the hallway. His laughter echoed back to her. Billy hadn't changed much since kindergarten, when he had given her a bracelet made of painted Cheerios. The crossing guard had told her mother, who had told the neighborhood, and by the end of the day, the whole world knew that five-year-old Rosie had a boyfriend. By six, the two of them were playing separately. By twelve, they barely knew each other.

Mr. Woo called Billy and Lauren's group first, which meant that Rosie's group was next. Billy Jones galloped through the doorway, looking like a clown with two squished toilet paper rolls that were supposed to be horns taped to the top of his baseball cap. One of them immediately flopped over on its side, reminding Rosie of her collapsed castle walls, except that Billy was onstage with no chance for an emergency trip to Home Depot.

"I'm *Pan*, and that's a *pan* in the neck!" said Billy, pulling the horn off his hat and tossing it in the wastepaper basket. "That's a pun," he added.

"Instead of 'pain in the neck,' get it? I'm God of the Shepherds, and you're not supposed to see me throwing one of my horns in the garbage can."

A smattering of giggles followed, and Billy, encouraged, said, "Pretend that I have two horns on my head, please. Oh, and I have the legs of a goat!" He lifted up his pant leg with a flourish, and down its side he had written "GOAT'S FEET!"

The class started laughing, and there was a chorus of shrill whistles. Mr. Woo stood up, saying, "I can't grade them if I can't hear them!"

Lauren burst into the room, saying, "I am a wood nymph!" She ran past Billy, who took off after her, galloping strangely. He pulled a stick out of his pocket and tapped it on Lauren's shoulder as if he were a fairy godmother turning her into a princess. "Poof!" said Billy. "You're a reed."

Lauren stopped and stood like a statue, her hands jammed to her sides.

"That's where the expression *reed-thin* comes from!" said Billy. "Now I'm inventing a shepherd's pipe out of reeds." He pulled a child's recorder out of his pocket and started playing a squeaky "Three Blind Mice." The audience squealed and plugged their ears.

Tommy Stone entered the room, wearing a dress

and a long red wig. "Hellooooo!" he cried, pretending to be mesmerized by Billy's music. He danced and wiggled so outrageously that Lauren the reed collapsed laughing.

"Hey, reed, do your job and stand up straight!" said Billy, pointing at her. "I have to run and get the other wood nymph!" He chased after Tommy, who ran frantically around the perimeter of the desks, his wig nearly flying off his head, crying, "I'm running from Pan because I'm in a *panic*!"

Billy turned to the class and said, "Get it? I've sent him into a *panic*! Pan. Panic. Mr. Woo, that's why I'm famous? I make people panic? It sucks. I mean, I'm the cause of sudden fear for no reason at all?"

"I think you're a panic," said Mr. Woo, smiling.

"Thank you," said Billy, turning quickly toward Lauren and growling so loudly that she screamed. "See? That was unrehearsed. And that's where we get the term *panic attack*." He galloped off to applause.

Rosie was beginning to panic herself. If Lauren's skit was ending, her group was up next!

Suddenly Tommy reappeared, making whinnying noises and flapping a pair of white feathered wings. "I'm Pegasus!" he called out.

64

Billy waved his arms and said, "Mr. Woo knew we'd be the best in the class, so he gave us *two* myths."

Tommy took over. "I was born from the bloooooooood of Medusa when her head was chopped off by Perseus." Billy rolled a Barbie doll head across the floor, and Tommy cried in a baby voice, "I want my mama, I want my mama." Lauren laughed louder than everyone else. It reminded Rosie of her own laughter at the rehearsal with Robbie, and her mother's happiness at a single phone call. What was it about boys that made girls act that way?

"Two minutes!" Mr. Woo pointed at Rosie, who scrambled into the hallway with her costume in a bag.

Teresa jumped up, script in hand, and began narrating before Rosie had slipped her fruity dress over her clothes. Robbie joined her and said, "Very fetching," an old-fashioned word that surprised Rosie. Mary must have left the classroom early. She was waiting in the hall, looking every inch the goddess in full makeup, a rhinestone tiara, and what appeared to be a new prom dress from Jessica McClintock or Betsey Johnson.

Teresa was calling from the classroom,

"Where's my wife, Demeter, De Mutter of my child?"

Rosie ran in, her fruit dress ballooning behind her. Mary followed, and began pulling a bush out of the concrete floor. Robbie galloped into the room on a hobbyhorse. Before long, the class was howling as much as they had for Billy and Lauren's skit. Then Robbie hooked an arm around Mary's neck, saying, "I'm abducting you and taking you to my kingdom," knocking her tiara down over her eyes.

"Hey!" said Mary. "You're choking me!" The tiara clattered across the floor and Mary chased after it, shrieking loudly as Robbie's foot anchored her dress to the spot. There was a ripping sound, and Mary's face was a picture of horror. "You've torn it!" she said between clenched teeth.

"That's not part of the script," said Robbie, deadpan, gallantly trying to hide the shredded edge of the dress by tucking it underneath her.

"Now I can't take it back to the store!" hissed Mary, whipping the ripped dress away from him.

Rosie was happier than she'd been in days.

Teresa chanted, "Let us continue. Later, in the kingdom of the underworld, Persephone plays jacks with the rubies and diamonds that Hades showers her with . . ."

A pouting Mary sat on the floor in her prom dress, her tiara jammed back on her head, bouncing a ball and picking up bunches of Teresa's fake jewels. Robbie handed her an apple, saying, "Make believe it's a pomegranate!" Mary pulled six gummy bears out of her pocket and started eating them, saying woodenly, "I love these pomegranate seeds."

"That means we're married," said Robbie, making a face, which made Rosie so ecstatic that she forgot to weep and wail. "Hey!" hissed Robbie. "How about some noises, Mom?"

"Oh!" Rosie proceeded to rant and rave and run around the room while Teresa said, "Demeter punished the earth's inhabitants with bitter cold and blustering winds. Unless Persephone is returned to her side, the earth will perish."

"No fair!" cried Billy. "I only give panic attacks to people! She destroys the earth!"

"Quiet, Pan," said Robbie, howling alongside Rosie.

Mary said darkly, "You're not supposed to side with Demeter, dope!"

Robbie said, "Sorry! I thought I'd help out De Mutter because De Fodder isn't doing much."

Teresa threw up her hands and said, "I'm narrating!" She could barely get out the words with all the laughter. "Finally, it was agreed that Persephone would spend part of the year with her husband, Hades, and part of the year with her mother, Demeter. Thus we have the division of the seasons. The sweetness of spring . . . and the harshness of winter. Cast, take a bow!"

Mary bent low, her hand anchoring her tiara to her blond head. "My dress!" she whispered. "I think the zipper broke!"

"It wasn't me!" said Robbie, looking down at his feet to make sure.

She hooked her arm behind her and, with a look of pure disbelief on her face, tried to pull the back of her split dress together. "Someone help me!" she cried.

In an instant, Rosie stepped behind Mary and held the two sides together so that the whole dress didn't fall off. "The division of the dress symbolizes the division of the seasons," she said.

Teresa jumped forward so quickly that her pom-poms quivered. She continued, "Yes, that's symbolism. The sweetness of spring and the harshness of winter!"

Robbie joined in. "Yes, I mean, would you like

to split your dress in front of the entire class? That's what I'd call *harsh*!"

The class started clapping, and the four of them took a bow, Rosie behind Mary, holding the dress together as if her life depended on it.

"Very inventive," said the teacher, wryly. "Get out of your costumes and join us back in the class-room."

As they were leaving the room, Rosie stepped on Robbie's heel. This time, she was smart enough not to ask if she'd hurt him.

"You were great," she said.

"You were cute," said Robbie, turning away from her.

"Excuse me?" said Rosie, in a state of shock, not believing her own ears, but he had walked into the boys' bathroom and was gone.

Did he really say what Rosie thought he'd said? Rosie stood stock-still in the middle of the hallway, very much like Lauren in her skit.

Teresa whispered in her ear, "I heard him. He said you were cute."

"Oh!" said Rosie, blushing. "Thanks a lot!"

"No problem," said Teresa, and Rosie realized that there wasn't a single problem in her life right now, because the sun was shining and the project was over, and Robbie had told her she was cute.

When she got home, Rosie wrote in her diary:

Wednesday

Dear Diary,

I know it's silly, but I'm hopeful again, because today, Robbie said that I was cute. Maybe he meant that I was cute in the play, but it doesn't matter. Cute wipes away Goldtwit if you ask me. Cute is great. Maybe I won't be decrushifying just yet. I am,

Yours truly,
Rosie Gold-better-and-better

P.S. So far, this hasn't been a kissing diary. Stay tuned . . .
P.P.S. What is it about the boys we like that makes us laugh harder at their silly jokes? I'll have to think about that one.

7

Rosie Goldglitt's Grandpa Joe

Dinner that evening was a Goldglitt lovefest for Rosie, Jimmy, and their mother. Rosie amused them by describing her skit over forkfuls of spaghetti and tofu meatballs. Her brother hooted when she told them about holding Mary's dress together.

"There would have been more drama if you'd let it fall to the floor," he said.

Mrs. Goldglitt congratulated Rosie. "You don't even like the girl, but you helped her out! I'm proud of you, honey. Love thine enemy," she said, rolling her eyes to heaven, which set them all laughing.

"She didn't even thank me," Rosie said. "Nothing changed. But Robbie said I was cute!"

"Did he say it sarcastically?" Jimmy asked.

"Not at all!" Nothing could sink Rosie's spirits

tonight. She had looked up the word *cute* in the dictionary. The definition sounded even better than the word itself. Robbie thought she was "endearingly pretty," and there hadn't been a hint of sarcasm.

They cleared the dirty dishes, and Jimmy surprised them by wiping off the table, a chore that he hated. Rosie and Jimmy did their homework in the living room and then settled down to watch television. Jimmy laughed at the he-man parts, and Rosie and her mother watched what the stars were wearing. The popcorn was salty, low-fat but tasty. For the first time in a long time, it felt like the family was working again.

The telephone rang, and Mrs. Goldglitt answered. By the look on her face, someone had died.

"Who's hurt?" said Rosie, remembering the same expression when the police had called to tell them that their father had been involved in a traffic accident.

"Who's dead?" said Jimmy, voicing what she felt.

"No one," their mother quickly replied, cupping her hand over the receiver. "Uncle Moe says there's something the matter with Grandpa. Let me hear."

Mrs. Goldglitt adored her father's brother. When Grandma Rebecca had ended up in the nursing home after a broken hip, Uncle Moe had come to the rescue. Rosie's parents were in the middle of their divorce, and Grandpa Joe didn't know how to make his bed, or pay the bills, or do the laundry. They all knew that Grandpa couldn't live by himself. But who could take him? Rosie's mother hated to see her father in a nursing home, but had put him on the waiting list to join Grandma Rebecca, just in case. Uncle Moe took pity and invited Grandpa to live with him until Grandma recovered. Rosie remembered hearing her mother tell her uncle, "I could kiss your feet, I'm so relieved." Twice a week, Uncle Moe had taken Grandpa to the nursing home to visit his wife. And one day, Grandma's bed was empty. She had died in the middle of the night.

Rosie loved Grandpa Joe better than anyone. Before the divorce, he was her biggest admirer. He listened to her. After Grandma died, with her mother dating and Jimmy in his own world and Dad building a new life away from them, Rosie needed Grandpa's ears more than ever. He rarely gave her much advice, but nodded his head or widened his eyes so that she felt understood. When Grandma was around, he had laughed a lot, as if the world's problems didn't touch him and life was expected to be good. After her death, the laughter had lessened.

Rosie's mother pressed the telephone against her ear, muttering, "I see, I see," over and over. When she said goodbye, she sank into the armchair with a sigh that wiped out the evening's pleasure. "Grandpa Joe is too much for Uncle Moe," she said. "He needs a break."

"For how long?" asked Rosie.

"He's not staying in my room," Jimmy said quickly.

"Jimmy, you'll have to sleep in Dad's old office. Your room is away from the stairs and next to the bathroom. We can't have Grandpa falling and breaking his neck." Mrs. Goldglitt's tone was flat and final.

"He has a sketchy smell!" Jimmy complained bitterly. "I don't want my bed smelling old like Grandpa."

"That's awful!" said Rosie, bristling at her brother.

"Then let him sleep in your bed!" said Jimmy, which shut Rosie up.

Mrs. Goldglitt walked out of the room muttering, "Do the laundry," and the subject was closed.

After school on Friday, Rosie and her mother drove to Uncle Moe's house. Summer wanted to come along for the ride, but Mrs. Goldglitt said no. "She's a lovely girl, but we don't need her chirping in the backseat, honey." Rosie didn't argue. Jimmy said Summer was like Chinese food. It filled you up for the moment, but you were hungry an hour later.

When Uncle Moe and Grandpa Joe walked out to greet them, Rosie's mother let out a deep shuddery sound that signaled disaster. "He's aged so much, I can't believe it! I just saw him a week ago!"

"He looks like he's going to fall down," said Rosie, noting how firmly Uncle Moe gripped his brother's elbow.

Grandpa shuffled his way toward them as if he were crippled. His face was pale, and his eyes were dead. It chilled Rosie to the bone. Uncle Moe helped him into the front seat of the car. Grandpa struggled with his seat belt until he got so exasperated that he wouldn't wear it. He didn't answer when Rosie said hello.

Rosie exchanged glances with her mother in the rearview mirror. Her mother's face was drained of color, in spite of carefully applied blush. Rosie knew what her mother was thinking: that Grandpa Joe looked as though he was ready to join his dear departed wife.

When they parked in the driveway, Rosie helped Grandpa out of the car.

"Where am I?" he said. "I want to go home."

"You're staying with us for a while, Grandpa."

Rosie and her mother led him as if they were guiding a sleepwalking child.

Rosie sat next to her grandfather on the couch. He didn't move or speak, but when she turned on the television, he directed his empty gaze at the set. She left him alone and went into the kitchen.

Rosie's mother wasn't much of a cook, but she'd managed to make her father roast beef, which sat like a bomb in her nearly vegetarian kitchen.

"We're eating flesh tonight?" Rosie joked. Her mother laughed, but it was thin and fake, coming from the windpipe, not the heart or the stomach. Jimmy and Rosie loved to make her laugh so hard that she was red in the face, with tears running down her cheeks. Each of them competed to be her favorite funny person. Lately, Sam topped everyone.

Grandpa wandered in, startling them both. He munched on a carrot, which made Rosie happy. Wanting to eat was being alive, wasn't it? He pulled Rosie to him, and said, "How's my little Rosebush?" Her real Grandpa was back as if she'd suddenly switched radio stations from classical to rock, asking about school and teachers and whether she had a nice boyfriend. When her mother announced, "Rosie likes to make her boyfriends fall head over heels backward into the bushes," they laughed too hysterically, relieved that Grandpa was feeling better. He demanded to hear the entire story, and drank a full glass of cream soda, bought especially for him.

"After weeks of torture, Robbie thinks I'm cute," Rosie told him.

"Cute? Not good enough." Grandpa wrinkled up his brow in mock anger, saying, "You're gorgeous. You're beautiful. Dump that bozo!"

"He's not a bozo, Grandpa. Boys my age don't say you're beautiful." Rosie giggled. "Besides, the dictionary says cute means 'endearingly pretty.' "

"Okay," he said grudgingly. "Endearingly pretty in an extraordinary way. That's my little Rosebush." He looked around the kitchen, saying, "Just the way I like it! A little bit of dirt. A little bit of clutter. Everything at Moe's is covered in plastic. One day, he's going to spray disinfectant on me."

"He's a neat freak like Sarah's mother," said Rosie, laughing. Maybe Grandpa had been lonely and just needed company. Her mother was smiling, and Rosie could talk about Robbie again without feeling bad.

The next day, Mrs. Goldglitt had to go to work. "Can you go for a walk with Grandpa?" she asked. "The fresh air and exercise will do him good. I'd take him, honey, but Saturday is such a busy day at work, and I took off two weeks ago. Besides, it's just a few hours."

"Can I wash my hair first?" Rosie asked, and her mother agreed. Sometimes Robbie and his friends hung around with their bicycles outside Sal's Pizzeria. Bumping into him with dirty hair wouldn't do. She was drying her hair with her head upside down when Grandpa called in to her, "I'm going for a short walk around the block! I'll come back and get you."

"I'm almost done!" she called back to him, swinging her head upright so fast it made her light-headed. She heard the door slam.

Ten minutes later, Grandpa wasn't back. Rosie stood outside and waited ten more, and then another ten before she started worrying. Should she call her mother and get yelled at when he might turn up at any moment? Rosie decided against it. She grabbed her jean jacket, dabbed some lip gloss on her mouth, and set off into town.

It was a ten-block stretch into the main part of town. Rosie peered down each intersection, looking for Grandpa. She passed Mr. Kerry, stooped but sturdy, who walked his dog several times a day. "Have you seen an old man?"

Mr. Kerry bristled. "What kind of old man? Is he fifty? Eighty? Be specific."

"Seventy," she told him.

"Young," said Mr. Kerry. "What was he wearing?"

"I'm not sure," Rosie said uncertainly.

"I haven't seen anyone matching that wonderful description."

Now, *that* was sarcastic, Rosie thought, walking off quickly.

She was getting tired and frightened. Was he lost, or worse, had he been hit by a car? She looked inside every store along the way, the bakery where her mother bought carrot muffins, the post office, the pharmacy, Sal's Pizzeria. No glimpse of Grandpa, no Robbie and his friends, just strangers going about their business.

"Rosie!"

It was a young male voice. Rosie looked around. Where was it coming from? Across the street and up the road, a boy darted into traffic, skirting cars and bounding toward her with a familiar gait. It was Billy Jones. His face was flushed, and he was breathing hard by the time he reached her.

"Come with me," he said, pulling her by the hand into oncoming traffic, weaving his way back to the bench where her grandfather sat.

"Here she is, sir," said Billy, and Grandpa's face lit up and a tear slid down his cheek.

"It's you!" said Grandpa, holding out a trembling hand. "I thought I'd lost you."

Rosie sat down next to him and cradled his hand in hers. "I'm here," she said. "It's okay, Grandpa."

Billy said, in a low voice, "I found him standing here, looking kind of confused, you know? At first, I thought he was drunk or something, he looked so out of it."

"He's not drunk!" Rosie said defensively.

"I know, I know! That's what I'm saying! I got him to sit down, and we started talking, and he says, 'I took a walk and I got lost and I'm looking for my little rosebush.' So I'm thinking, okay, he lives in a house with roses around it, but it's too early for the roses to be out yet, you know? Then I remember Mrs. Petrie has that rosebush that twines all over the picket fence, around the corner from the school, and he gets agitated, and he's shaking his head, and he says, 'No! No! My little rosebush, I need my little rosebush,' and he's looking around, and his face lights up, and he says, 'There she is!' And it was you."

Rosie couldn't speak.

Billy rushed on, saying, "So I said, you mean her? Rosie? Is that your little Rosebush? And he said yes."

"He called me that when I was a little girl."

"I wondered." Billy paused, and turned toward Grandpa. He spoke clearly in his ear. "So you've found your granddaughter, sir!"

"Yes," said Grandpa, squeezing Rosie's hand.

"Do you want to come home with me?" Rosie said.

"I'll walk you there," said Billy. He stood up, and Rosie recognized the familiar Billy smell that cried out for a shower. Today, it was cologne, it was perfume, it was Mrs. Petrie's roses at their very best, because Billy was her knight in shining armor.

They walked, the three of them, Grandpa in the middle, until they reached Rosie's house.

Her mother's car was in the driveway. Billy helped her grandfather up the stairs. His steps were slow and labored, as if each one cost him a year or two.

"Thank you so much," Rosie whispered to Billy, thinking his blue eyes were so kind that they made her want to cry.

"You're late!" said her mother, fussing around them, looking quizzically at Billy.

"He got lost," Rosie told her, gesturing toward Grandpa, watching her mother's face turn grave. "Billy found him."

Mrs. Goldglitt started grilling them as if she were a police detective. After a few minutes, Billy said that his mother must be wondering what had happened to him. "I was supposed to bring back milk for her coffee!" he said.

Rosie's mother thanked him with tears in her eyes. Billy shifted from foot to foot, saying, "It's okay. It's really okay."

Rosie walked him to the door. "Do you want some milk?" she said, feeling awkward.

"I'm not thirsty," he said, turning the doorknob.

Rosie couldn't help laughing. "For your mother!"

"Oh!" Billy hit the side of his head. "No, that's okay, I'll go buy a quart," he called over his shoulder.

"What a good boy," Mrs. Goldglitt said when Rosie joined her.

"He makes me laugh," said Rosie.

For the rest of the visit, they never left Grandpa alone, and there was very little laughter. Mrs. Goldglitt took Grandpa to the doctor for tests, and he told her that Grandpa would not be getting better and shouldn't be left alone.

Mr. Goldglitt arrived to help take Grandpa to the nursing home. They sat around the table until it was time to go.

"You got along with Grandpa, didn't you, Dad?" Rosie asked.

"He was good to me. He treated me like a son." His eyes darted sideways toward Rosie's mother as if she might make a comment. "Even after we told him we were getting divorced."

"He loved you," said Mrs. Goldglitt grimly. "Thank goodness I put him on the list for the nursing home. How could I ever take care of him?"

But Rosie saw a look in her mother's eyes, the

look of guilt and pain that said: A good daughter would take him. A good daughter wouldn't make him live with strangers for the rest of his life.

"He doesn't know us anymore," said Rosie, defending her. "He's there but he's not."

Rosie's mother sipped the last of her coffee. "I wish I could do it," she said quietly. "I'm an orphan now."

"You have us," said Jimmy.

Rosie looked at her mother, wrinkles fanning out from her dark-shadowed eyes. Her father looked older, running his hand through hair that used to be thicker. Rosie didn't want to be an orphan any time soon.

"We should go," said her father, walking into the living room to help Grandpa off the couch. "Let me carry your bag, Pop," he said, gently prying the satchel away from the old man.

"Where am I going?"

Nobody answered, and Grandpa didn't ask again. Perhaps he had forgotten the question. Mr. Goldglitt handed Rosie the satchel and helped Grandpa up with two hands. It was as if Grandpa had forgotten how to bend his legs, how to sit down, how to talk, and, especially for Rosie, how to listen.

Rosie went to bed early that evening. The Kissing Diary seemed a little silly, next to death and dying. It made Rosie wonder if she really wanted to get old, with all the sorrow that led up to it. She read the last entry before Grandpa's arrival, so light and breezy, so full of hope!

But the clean blank page beckoned Rosie to fill it, and she wrote:

Sunday evening

I miss Grandpa already.

I am yours,
Rosie Gold-sadder
. . . and . . . sadder . . . and . . . sadder

8

Rosie's Mind over What-Mary-Says-Doesn't-Matter

As soon as she saw Billy running up the steps to school on Monday morning, Rosie knew she had to help him. "Billy!" she called.

He continued bounding down the hallway.

"Billy!" she cried. He kept on walking. "BILLY!" she screamed so loudly that everyone stared at her. *That's my last time,* she said to herself, feeling ridiculous. He stopped.

Rosie ran to meet him and put a hand on his shoulder, saying, "Turn around."

"What is it?" Billy did as he was told.

Rosie peeled a pair of pink thong underwear off the back of his sweatshirt. "You didn't mean to wear these, did you?" she whispered, handing them to him.

"Oh, man!" Billy rolled them into a ball and

stuck them deep in his book bag. His face turned beet red, and he mumbled, "Sometimes the dryer does that, you know? Static electricity. They're my sister's!"

"I didn't think they were yours," said Rosie.

"Thanks," said Billy. "I owe you one. I'll see you later in history class."

She headed in the opposite direction, and someone called out, "Nice save, Rosie!"

Teresa was grinning widely at her. "He's not the pink thong type, is he?"

"Not really!" said Rosie.

"He'd be cute if he wore some deodorant!" said Teresa, jingling cheerfully as she walked.

Rosie agreed. "Wouldn't you think his friends would say something?"

"Half his friends don't shower!" said Teresa, and they walked into homeroom laughing.

In Mrs. Geller's class, Rosie sat down at her desk, watching her teacher's butt shake as she wrote on the blackboard. Someone should show her a video of her backside in jiggly motion. Maybe that was why her mother used the elliptical trainer so religiously.

"Hello," said Robbie, clearly, audibly, directed at her. She nearly fell off her chair.

"Hi," she answered, searching for something clever to say.

"How was your weekend?"

"Good. We put my grandfather in a nursing home."

"That's good?"

"No," said Rosie hastily, "that's bad. We had to do it. He got lost in town."

"You put him in a nursing home for getting lost in town?" Robbie whistled.

"*No!* It's not like that!" Rosie spoke rapidly. "When my grandmother died, he was on the waiting list at the home, but Mom didn't want him to go, and Uncle Moe took him in, but then he started going downhill and he got lost in town. That's when we knew for sure that he was sick." *Too much information,* Rosie said to herself. *Muzzle! Muzzle!*

Robbie didn't seem to care. "Hey, my mom's always losing things," he said. "I found her checkbook in the freezer last night when I was getting some ice cream."

Rosie giggled. What should she say next? *Think cute! Think CUTE!*

Before she could respond, Robbie said, "So,

have you tried the new ice cream place next to Sal's?"

Her heart did a flip-flop. Was he going to ask her to try it with him? "Not yet," said Rosie, thinking she should have said, "Want to go sometime?"

"Open up your textbooks to page 278," Mrs. Geller interrupted, and their conversation was over. Rosie wanted to banish her teacher to the underworld, but less than an hour later, she sailed out of the classroom in a buzz of happiness.

After school, Lauren was excited as well. "Tommy Stone poked me in the ribs today twice! On the way into class, and on the way out."

"Great!" said Rosie. "Robbie might have been asking me to go for ice cream!"

"Might have?" Lauren said, widening her eyes.

"Might have," said Rosie, and they burst into laughter. "We're pathetic, aren't we?"

"We are!" said Lauren. "I'll call you when I get back from the orthodontist's."

"What's for dinner?" Rosie called after her. "*Ribs?*" She could hear Lauren cackling as she walked down the street.

When Rosie got home, her mother was folding laundry and watching a talk show on TV. She gestured with her chin at the television screen. "Look at Faith Hill. She sings. She's gorgeous. Great skin and hair, a romantic husband. They don't even have a nanny, can you believe that? And she cooks, too! What is she, superwoman?"

Rosie sat next to her. "Maybe she looks normal when she's not on television. Maybe she yells. Maybe she has a cleaning woman. Or dimples on her thighs."

Her mother sighed. "She feels blessed when she wakes up in the morning, Rosie. When I wake up, I just feel tired." She pulled some clothes out of the laundry basket. "How are you, honey?"

Rosie said, "Actually, I'm great! Robbie and I had a conversation today. Can you believe it?"

"It's a miracle," said Mrs. Goldglitt, putting the socks in a pile.

"Don't be mean," Rosie said.

"I meant to be funny." She pointed to the pile of clothes in the basket. "Help me."

Rosie folded a pair of jeans. "It's the first time he's really spoken to me since he said I was cute!"

"You are cute. And smart. No one needs to tell

you that. You should know. Did Mrs. Geller grade our castle yet?"

"We got a B," said Rosie, holding up a pair of trousers. "Are these Jimmy's?"

"Yes. The Jimmy pile is on the coffee table. It's very small, because most of his dirty clothes are in his room, on the floor."

"He's a slob," said Rosie, reaching for a shirt that she knew was hers.

"And your room is better?" Her mother raised an eyebrow.

Rosie ignored her and said, "So he asked me if I'd tried the new ice cream shop in town."

"Really!" Mrs. Goldglitt lined up one sock with another and rolled them into a ball. "So I may be right, Miss Rosie. He likes you."

"Maybe." Rosie wanted her mother's theory to be true, more than anything. "Mrs. Geller ruined the moment by talking."

Mrs. Goldglitt laughed. "Don't you mean teaching?"

"Whatever. She started jabbering about Marco Polo."

"As long as she didn't give you a weekend project. I want to visit Grandpa."

Rosie felt a wash of sadness. "Do I have to go?"

"I'm not going to make you." Her mother stood up abruptly and looked in the mirror on the living room wall. "I hope this business with Grandpa isn't going to make me lose my hair."

Rosie observed her mother, who had been moping about Grandpa for days. "It doesn't look any thinner." Even if it had, Rosie wouldn't have told her. Why make her feel worse, anyway? When Grandma had died, and her parents were getting divorced, her mother's hair started falling out in clumps. The doctor had told her it was stress-related, and it freaked her mother out. His wife, the receptionist, recommended taking yoga.

"Do your mantra," Rosie told her mother.

"I've lost it somewhere." Mrs. Goldglitt shook her head. "Can you imagine? I've lost my mantra."

"I think you lost it when you started seeing Sam," said Rosie.

"Could be," said her mother, breaking into a smile.

Her mother's mantra had been written down on an index card by her spiritual adviser. Rosie remembered hearing her chant it through the bedroom wall, something like *"Ombody ohbody almighty umbody,"* over and over.

Rosie had found the card one day when she was borrowing a necklace from her mother's bureau. She tried reading it aloud, but her mother came running and snatched it out of her hand. "*Don't do that!* It's my own private mantra. If anyone else repeats it, it loses its power!"

Rosie turned away from Faith Hill and her mother. "Are we done?" she said, and her mother nodded.

It was time to invent a mantra for herself. Rosie sat on her bed and began chanting, "*I am cute I am cute Robbie thinks so I am cute I am cute I am cute I believe that I am cute.*" She looked in the mirror and repeated it. Her face was shining. She smiled at herself. She chanted once more. Her eyes were glowing. Maybe the mantra was working.

On Saturday, Lauren, Summer, Sarah, and Rosie hung out together. They had their own routine, walking to the local drugstore, which had a lot of cool jewelry and a ton of makeup. Afterward, they would eat a slice of pizza at Sal's next door. Rosie suggested they try the new ice cream shop, and the girls nodded knowingly.

Summer found a lip gloss she liked right away. She bought two of them, which made Rosie feel jealous. Summer never had to worry about money, and often bought doubles: two T-shirts in different colors, two pairs of pants, two bracelets. Summer's mother let her wear lipstick, mascara, and blush. Rosie's mother only allowed colorless lip gloss. "I might as well be wearing Vaseline," Rosie protested, knowing that back in the Vaseline ages, her mother had worn exactly that. Summer convinced Lauren to buy a cool-looking Mocha Peony. She painted a line of Cherry Malt on her wrist, saying, "This one has your name on it, Rosie."

Rosie smeared a dab of it on her own hand. It was pale pink with a wisp of mocha and cream. It looked good enough to eat.

"I think you can get away with that one," said Summer. "Your mother won't mind."

"Robbie will think you're even cuter," whispered Lauren, in case someone was lurking nearby who shouldn't hear.

Rosie appreciated Lauren's good sense. Her mantra drifted through her head: *I am cute I am cute Robbie thinks so I am cute I am cute I am cute I believe that I am cute.* She bought it immediately.

"Let's help Sarah now," said Summer.

"It's hopeless," said Sarah. "My mother only

wants me to wear natural products. She's afraid these were tested on dogs or something."

"I've never seen a dog wearing lipstick," said Summer.

"Ruff ruff," said Lauren. "That means, let's eat!"

There was something about hooting hysterically in public that made the girls feel happy and popular. They did just that, and left the shop with their purchases to go eat pizza at Sal's.

Rosie's nickname for Sal was Mr. Grouch. They ordered their slices and grabbed bunches of napkins, dabbing at the oil until the table was littered with paper. Sal glowered at them as if they'd started a raging forest fire. When Sarah gathered up the napkins and threw them in the garbage, he said, "What a waste." Pulling a small packet of baby wipes out of her purse, Sarah took one out and polished the table. "All clean," she announced, checking to see if Sal's frown had changed. It hadn't. "I tried," she said. The girls finished their pizza and pulled out their lipsticks, applying Mocha Peony and Pink Powderpuff and Cherry Malt, pouting in the pizza parlor mirror.

It was a grand day for Rosie, out with the girls, no boys to bother them, no mothers worrying about losing their hair or yelling about something. Just the four of them. Today, Rosie loved them more than anything. She would wear the glossy new lipstick to school on Monday with her mantra humming inside her head.

"What's it like kissing a boy when you're wearing lip gloss?" Rosie asked Summer, who had done it once.

"You wipe it off if you think it might happen," Summer advised.

"Does the boy care?" Rosie wondered.

"I think some of them do, and some of them don't," Sarah gave her opinion. "I would mind."

"Because you're a clean freak," Summer said, watching her friend deposit their paper plates in the receptacle.

"What if the guy ate mint chocolate chip ice cream before he kissed you?" Rosie mused. "Mint makes me want to hurl!"

"What if he hates the taste of mocha chocolate chip?" Lauren said, laughing. "That's your favorite!"

"You'll grin and bear it," said Sarah.

"Is Robbie a virgin kisser, do you think?" The minute the words were out of Rosie's never-been-kissed-by-a-boy mouth, Mary Katz walked in. Rosie shushed them and said, "Hi, Mary!"

Mary spoke to Sal. "I'm picking up the order for Katz," she said, giving Rosie what could only be called a semi-smile.

"Aren't you glad the Greek skit is over?" Rosie kept her voice friendly.

"Hey, I'm sure *you're* happy!" Mary said, animated. "At least I was wearing a prom dress, you know? You were stuck looking like a big bowl of fruit salad. Robbie had me in stitches, we thought it was so funny! I almost wet myself!" Her smile was so malicious it took Rosie's breath away.

Lauren, forever loyal, couldn't keep her mouth shut, saying, "He told her she looked cute."

"Too bad she doesn't know when someone is kidding!" Mary drummed her French-manicured fingers on the counter. "Is my broccoli rabe ready yet?"

"Nasty stuff," muttered Summer. "It smells so bad."

Rosie watched Mary sail out of the restaurant, her order in hand, the word *Juicy* emblazoned across her rear end. *Trust her to leave disaster in her path like a hurricane ripping through an entire town,* she thought.

"Don't even think about it," said Lauren.

"Don't believe her," Summer added.

"Zap it out of your head," Sarah said emphatically.

Rosie hugged her friends when they got to her block. She walked slowly past Mr. Slope's man-made pond with the fountain of water running out of Cupid's mouth, past the strip of flowers that Mrs. Goldberg tended, past the mailbox that Mrs. McCue had painted bright pink, past the house that had permanent Christmas lights. She repeated her mantra over and over. It soothed her. It healed her. She would not listen to Mary. She would wear her new lipstick on Monday morning. And when Robbie saw her, he would think she was cute again, because they'd talked for real and because she knew she was cute without anyone telling her.

Home at last, Rosie ran up the stairs and opened her diary. She kissed the blank page with her lips slightly parted. Underneath, she wrote:

Saturday

Rosie in her new Cherry Malt lipstick.

Then she added:

Mary tried to make me feel bad about myself today. I won't buy it. I won't wear it. I won't eat it either. Grandpa said I was beautiful. Mom says I'm smart. Dad says I'm both. I don't need anyone but me to believe it. I am so much better than a bowl of fruit.

I am also,

Yours sincerely,
Rosie Gold-getting-cuter-and-cuter

9

Rosie Wrestles with Reason

A mantra only works for so long, until real life hits you over the head. Early Saturday afternoon, a week later, Rosie was still lounging in her pajamas when her mother got back from visiting Grandpa.

Rosie could tell by her face that it hadn't gone well. Her mother looked as sad as Rosie had felt when she had knocked over a bucket of minnows at the creek, and couldn't save them. "How's Grandpa?" Rosie asked, steeling herself, remembering the tiny fish flipping and dying at the edge of the water.

"He thought I was still married to Dad, poor thing. But he recognized me, which was a blessing. So the nurse said I could take him out to lunch, that he was having a good day."

"And?"

Mrs. Goldglitt plopped down next to Rosie on the couch. "He couldn't remember what he liked to eat, so I ordered him eggplant parmigiana. He used to love that. He ate it, but . . ." She stopped, at a loss for words.

"What? He didn't like it?"

"He eats so strangely. Very messy. Sauce is dripping on his shirt. He doesn't know when he has to wipe his mouth, you know?" Tears sprang to her eyes, and she continued. "Then I go to put him in the car, and he can't remember how to bend his knees. Can you imagine? This big tall man, and I'm trying to tell him how to bend his knees and put his head down so I can get him into the car."

"What did you do?"

"I managed, somehow. Or he remembered." She picked up the pillow next to her and peered at it. "Is this a chocolate stain?"

"Jimmy eats in here, too, you know! Go on, Mom. What happened?"

Mrs. Goldglitt shook her head and put the pillow down. "So I drive him back to the nursing home, and I get him out of the car, and he starts shouting, 'There's no bed for me at this hotel. I want to go home! Take me home. Take me home!' I was trying to soothe him, but what could I say?

'This awful place is where you'll live until you die'?"

"Oh, Mommy." It was Rosie's turn to get teary.

They were silent for a while. Suddenly her mother sprang up from the couch. "Enough of that. It's Saturday afternoon. You're going to the movies tonight, aren't you? I'm seeing Sam. No more crying! Come with me!" She took Rosie's hand and dragged her in her slippers through the dining room into the tiny bathroom off the kitchen. "Now look in the mirror," she instructed her.

Rosie stood cheek to cheek with her mother, two oval faces with a similar bone structure, her own green eyes flecked with bits of gold. Perhaps they were a little too deep-set and small, but she knew they were pretty without being told. Her mother's eyes were brown and soulful, framed by wrinkles that threatened to deepen.

"Now smile!" she commanded.

The two of them smiled, staring at their reflections. Rosie's face came alive, and her mother's wrinkles appeared to recede.

Rosie laughed. "Is there a space for us at the loony bin, Mom?" she said.

Mrs. Goldglitt put her arm around Rosie. "It's a

scientific fact that when you smile, and especially when you laugh, it triggers the release of chemicals called endorphins. It makes you feel better!"

"Do you feel better?" Rosie asked.

"I do. Do you?"

Rosie honestly did. She followed her mother into the kitchen. Her mother made a pot of coffee. Rosie told her about Mary's hurtful words.

Her mother said, "Far be it from me to pass judgment, Rosie, but that girl is evil!"

Rosie agreed. "I keep wondering what I ever did to hurt her! I mean, I saved her from standing in her bra and underwear in front of the whole class!"

"You may never know why she doesn't like you," said her mother. "But I can tell you this: Mary feels better by making people feel worse. We should pity her."

It was hard to pity a person who had everything: good looks, a big house, great clothes, lots of friends. She was even athletic. Couldn't Mary have inherited a flaw or two? Couldn't she suck at basketball? Either the gym teacher made Mary captain, or she was chosen first for a team. Mary didn't have a grandfather who forgot how to sit down.

Rosie left her mother and wandered upstairs. The thing about Mary was that she had so much power. Like the time she was eating lunch in the cafeteria. Every time a new person walked over with her tray, Mary said loudly, "I know, don't you hate her? What does she think she's doing in those boots? Shhh! She's coming, she'll hear you!" Everyone laughed, and someone else would arrive, and Mary started the game all over again with another judgment. What does she think she's doing in that skirt, with that nerd, with her hair in a ponytail, wearing knee socks? There was always laughter, from the crowd around Mary and even from the person who'd been dissed.

Rosie rearranged her line of stuffed animals. She repeated her mantra, trying to banish Mary's nastiness from her head.

She took out her diary and wrote:

Saturday afternoon

Dear Diary,

Did I get it wrong? Did Robbie say, you are a fruit, instead of you're cute? Was he being sarcastic, like Mary said? Oh, you're cute, real cute, you loser? Am I reading too much into everything? Am I losing my mind? No! Believe in yourself. Like Mom said, Mary is evil. She made the whole thing up, to bring me down. Because Robbie didn't have to talk to me in class the other day, or ask, out of the blue, if I'd tried the new ice cream shop. It makes me so mad that I doubt myself because of one evil person!

So here are my thoughts for the day. I know I'm very far from kissing Robbie, but I'm closer than before. There's nothing worse than being talked out of believing in yourself. Like the time I was in kindergarten and I splashed water down my pants at the water fountain and somebody said I'd peed in my pants, and I knew I hadn't. I absolutely, positively knew I hadn't. But everyone was telling the teacher that I had, and the teacher told my mother to bring dry clothes, and I never said to her, <u>But I did not pee in my pants!</u> My mother took me into the teeny tiny kindergarten bathroom and discovered that I wasn't wet at all. I remember she said, "You're bone-dry, honey," because it was a funny thing to say. And she said, "Why did you think you'd peed in your pants?" And I said, "They told me I did, so I believed them."

So. I'm not going to let Mary convince me

that Robbie didn't tell me I was cute or that
overnight I've lost my mind. It's like she's trying to
make me believe that I peed in my pants! The next
time anyone tries to ruin my day, I'm going to
look into the mirror and smile real wide, and let
those _endorfins?_ _endorphins?_ (however you spell
it)—anyway, I'll let them do their happiness thing.

I am yours,
Rosie Go-get-a-life-Mary-glitt

P.S. I still worry that I'd gag if Robbie ate
mint chocolate chip ice cream before he kissed me.
I guess that should be my worst problem.

10
Rosie Snaps

Rosie lay in bed wishing it weren't Monday morning. A whisper of sunlight trickled through her window. An alarm went off, and the noises began: a grunting sound as her mother rolled out of bed, slippers shuffling down the hallway, teeth being brushed, a splash of water. Then, "Jimmy! Rosie! Time to get up!" which made Rosie pull the covers up to her nose.

Her own morning noises had begun inside her head. Mary, Robbie, buzz buzz buzz. Mary, Robbie, buzz buzz buzz. Does he like me, does he not? Buzz buzz buzz. It made Rosie feel tired all over and want to snuggle down deeper under the blankets, but she made the momentous decision to shut the noises out. *No, no, triple no!* Mary Katz would not be allowed to operate the happiness button inside Rosie's head, and that was final.

She dressed for school in her favorite pink T-shirt with the strawberry ice cream cone on the front. She put on her best pair of jeans, the Steve Madden shoes that her father had bought her at the mall, and her Cherry Malt lip gloss. She smiled at her reflection in the full-length mirror on the door. Grandpa was right. The mirror didn't lie. Rosie Goldglitt looked better than cute.

She heard Jimmy bellowing about a pair of socks, and her mother bellowing back, *"In the clothes dryer!"* He glanced into her room, and caught her vamping as if she were a fashion model. Jimmy stuck out his butt and snaked his arms through the air, his mouth in a pout. Rosie surprised him by laughing instead of punching him in the arm.

"Big date at school?" her brother joked as they made their way down the stairs and into the kitchen.

"Nope," said Rosie. "I'm in a good mood." She poured herself a bowl of Corn Pops. *Hurrah for sugary cereal,* she thought, setting the box on the table for her morning read.

"So I see," said Jimmy, choosing Cap'n Crunch for himself.

Mrs. Goldglitt arrived, carrying a basket of laundry. "You're walking to school. I told you last night that my car is in the shop."

Rosie's brother didn't bother to wait for her. He put his bowl in the sink, slung his book bag over his shoulder, and shouted, "See you later!" as he slammed the door. Rosie knew the unspoken siblings rule. Older brothers didn't want to be seen with their younger sisters.

Mrs. Goldglitt leaned the basket on her hip. "He's so fast I couldn't yell at him to put his dish in the dishwasher. Where's he running to?"

"Maybe he has a date," said Rosie, surprising her mother by kissing her goodbye.

Rosie walked to school at a leisurely pace. She plucked a leaf off a neighbor's bush and snapped it in half. It made such a clean satisfactory sound that it made Rosie think of English class. Mr. Woo and his love of language. A shiny green leaf. What was the word? *Symbol*, that was it. The snapping of the leaf was a *symbol* of Rosie's morning decision. Crisp, new, starting over. *Snap.* She threw the leaf in the gutter and laughed out loud. Okay, now the leaf was crushed and discarded, but Rosie wasn't. *Holy cow,* she thought, smiling at the expression her mother used when she wasn't cursing. She was laughing and smiling and turning over a *new leaf,* that was it! The endorphins were working.

Lauren noticed. "You look beautiful!" she said, the way only a totally non-jealous friend can.

"You do too!" said Rosie happily, hooking arms with Lauren.

"I'm glad you're not letting Mary get to you."

"I refuse," said Rosie. "I know what I know. Robbie talks to me now. He doesn't hate me. Mary is nuts."

A block before they reached the school, Lauren stopped in her tracks. "Isn't that your brother with a girl?"

Rosie watched Jimmy as if he were a space alien. His eyes were closed, and he was kissing Linda Reeves in the shadow of the overhanging shrubbery, way better than Rosie remembered her mother kissing Sam. Slowly. Dreamily. Leisurely. Like Rosie's walk.

"That's why he rushed out of the house," said Rosie. "He'll be late for school."

"He doesn't seem to care," said Lauren, laughing. "She's very pretty!"

"I can't believe it!" Rosie answered, thinking if Jimmy could get the girl he liked, why couldn't she get Robbie? Too bad he was her brother. Asking Jimmy for tips on kissing would be way too weird! The bell rang, and Rosie and Lauren ran up the steps into school.

Rosie couldn't pinpoint where things started going wrong. She was sitting in English class listening to Lauren talk about the seventh-grade dance for the twentieth time. Should she ask Tommy Stone? Could she get up the nerve? Should they all go together, the four girls, instead? Rosie figured she should listen without complaining. After all, she had bombarded her friend with remarks like "Do you think Robbie likes me? Does he really think I'm cute?" over a thousand times. Lauren hadn't run off screaming once!

"Remember when I spoke to my brother about asking Tommy Stone?" said Rosie. "He said it's fine to ask a boy if you know he likes you. If he doesn't, you might not get the answer you want."

"That was so helpful," said Lauren, making a face. "Are we early, or is Mr. Woo late?"

Billy rushed past them, and Rosie felt like laughing. If she were making a cartoon character based on Billy, puffs of smoke would billow behind him, with BODY ODOR BOY written underneath. Her mother had a friend who drank too much alcohol, and her family and friends had held an intervention, with everyone telling her why they hated it when she drank. Maybe that was exactly what Billy needed. A body odor intervention. Rosie looked at Lauren, who wrinkled up her nose. She giggled and put her head in her hands. Billy turned and cast her a long glance with the clear blue eyes that had shone with kindness when he had helped Grandpa. How could she forget? Her giggling stopped. Maybe if she made an anonymous call to the Billy Jones household, it would help.

Just at that moment, Mr. Woo walked in, and Rosie nearly died because he sniffed the air and said out loud, "It smells funny in here. Did someone's lunch go bad?" Then Tommy breezed in, late as usual, and said, "Gag me with a spoon, what *is* that pong?" Everyone started laughing, and Tommy gathered steam, the center of attention and of Lauren's heart, and he called out, "Tell me it ain't you, Billy Boy! Tell me the *pong* ain't you!"

"It could be Rosie," Mary volunteered, her words actress-clear, as if she'd rehearsed the line

112

and intended it to be heard in the very last row.

Rosie was ready to die a second time. It was one thing having Billy ridiculed. Billy seemed to laugh it off. Rosie scribbled furiously in her English notebook, making a dark cloud of crisscross anger across the lined page.

Mary continued ruthlessly, saying, "It smells like rotten fruit or something, doesn't it? Rosie, weren't you fruit in a former life? *Yes!* You were fruity in our Greek skit!"

Rosie couldn't believe her ears. She tried to recall what her mother had said: Mary feels better by putting people down? But the wave of class laughter made her feel sick.

Billy said loudly, "It's not Rosie," and Mr. Woo added, "It certainly isn't. Rosie smells as sweet as her name." Then he quoted Shakespeare about a rose by any other name smelling as sweet, but the damage was done, because half the class was snickering, and a couple of people were flapping their arms and sniffing their armpits.

Rosie looked at Robbie, who had a smile on his face, flickering like a nasty little moth. Then and there, Rosie invented a brand-new mantra: *Mean Mary, Mean Mary, I hate Mean Mary,* but it didn't soothe her, and her endorphins scattered helplessly as if they'd run away.

Mr. Woo started his lesson, but Rosie could barely listen, and when the class was finally over, she had hardly taken a single note on plot and alliteration and onomatopoeia. Mercifully, the bell rang, and she was ready to flee, but Mary wasn't finished. She stood up with a big, fat smile on her pretty/ugly face. "You and Billy should go to the dance together," she said, enunciating beautifully so that the words rang across the room. "We could crown you Class Farts."

Rosie got to her feet, her books pressed to her chest. She slammed them down hard, and walked over to Mary, saying very clearly, "What have I ever done to you?"

"You exist," Mary answered, which was exactly the moment that Rosie hauled off and hit her in the face.

Mr. Woo saw it. Most of the class saw it. Mary felt it, and her nose started to bleed.

And with that single punch, Rosie felt her endorphins say goodbye and flee her body forever. Pffft. Gone.

Later, Rosie wrote in her diary:

Monday evening

Today, I completely lost it. My life is ruined. I hit Mary Katz in the face. I am so messed up. I have to sign this:

Rosie Gold-hitter

11

Rosie Goldglitt in the Pits

Rosie's father didn't believe in swearing, raising your voice, or using force. Her mother didn't believe in hitting either, but since she sometimes swore and often yelled, she couldn't preach against them too persuasively. When Rosie's class read about Mahatma Gandhi, Mr. Goldglitt gave a similar nonviolent lecture at supper that night. Rosie listened halfheartedly. School was over, and did they have to learn a lesson at dinnertime? She forgot about Gandhi when she shoved her brother in the kitchen after he cleared only the dishes that he had dirtied. How unfair was that, leaving Rosie with the rest? Her mother, however, didn't see it that way, and banished her to her room after she'd cleaned the whole kitchen. No hitting was at the top of the Goldglitt list of rules.

At the end of her parents' unraveling marriage, Rosie shut the door to the bedroom when she heard her mother begging for her father not to leave, that it would ruin the children, that she couldn't support them, that he was wrecking her life, that she hated him more than anything and should never have married him in the first place. It seemed as though the divorce was her mother's fault, with all the screaming and the shouting. Her father's voice was calm and quiet, as if he were narrating a movie about freshwater trout. Please don't raise your voice at me, Lucy. That's how the children get their potty mouths, Lucy. Take your hand off my arm, Lucy. Of course, it only infuriated her mother more. Mrs. Goldglitt became a stormer—storming out of the room, storming up the stairs, storming out of the house and into the car, where she would sit until she had simmered down. If she'd remembered to grab her car keys, she would start the ignition and put on the radio, listening with eyes closed. She didn't have a mantra yet. That was afterward. But if Rosie was honest, she might have admitted that her mother yelled less when her father was gone, which made Rosie think that becoming a yeller might have had something to do with her father.

On the fateful day that Rosie hit Mary, Mr. Goldglitt's advice to turn the other cheek flew out of her head. The Gandhi/Goldglitt philosophy slipped stealthily away. She knew what she'd done was wrong. She knew it was horrible. It felt almost like a reflex action, as if a doctor had hit her elbow instead of her knee, with a little rubber hammer that made her hand slap Mary.

The very worst thing for Rosie, next to facing her mother, was the look Mr. Woo had given her. He'd been punched in the stomach without any warning. If Mr. Woo had become her favorite teacher, Rosie felt as though she was his favorite student. It thrilled her when he'd written across the top of her paper, "Rosie, you have such an original voice. You're a star!" It was hard finding people who thought you were a star. Grandma Rebecca was dead. Grandpa was half-dead. Her mother was dating and dressing like a teenager. Her father was building a new life with a wife who didn't yell. Not yet, anyway. Calling Rosie a star wasn't part of his vocabulary, unless she got straight A's on her report card or something. Just a month ago, Mr. Woo had handed back an essay, saying, "Another flash of Rosie brilliance," for all the world to hear. It had made her day.

Then, out of the blue, his favorite student had hauled off and hit Mary Katz in the face. Rosie could almost see herself being plucked out of the constellation by Mr. Woo and flung into space. Rosie Goldglitt, falling star, crashing to the ground.

Immediately after she had committed her crime, Rosie's eyes darted from Mary's bloody nose to Mr. Woo's warm brown disappointed eyes. He said, "Hitting is not tolerated, Rosie. You give me no choice. Please go to the principal's office and tell him what happened. Lauren, take Mary to the nurse's office."

Lauren glanced at her friend briefly and steered Mary down the hallway as if she were Rosie's grandfather not remembering how to walk.

Rosie felt as though she were starring in her very own prison movie, sentenced to death and dragging herself to the electric chair. Mrs. Collins, the school secretary, instructed Rosie to sit inside the principal's office and wait for his return. Mr. Dosher's desk was full of photographs of his smiling children and his devoted wife. His wife looked slim in her wedding gown, and as the line of pictures progressed, she got fatter and fatter. The children hit the awkward stage, a teenaged girl trying to hide a mouth full of braces, a sullen boy looking as though he didn't want to smile at all. There was even a picture of a grinning dog. When Mr. Dosher walked through the door, he wasn't smiling. Rosie's heart pounded wildly, and she tried focusing her attention on the collie's pink wet tongue instead of the principal's turned-down mouth.

"I'm surprised to see you here, Rosie," he began.

"Me too," Rosie answered.

"Can you tell me what happened?" Mr. Dosher adjusted one of the framed pictures as if he suspected someone had moved it. "I just saw Mary in the nurse's office, and she says you gave her a bloody nose for no reason at all!"

"I guess," said Rosie. Why was her voice so trembly and high?

"You guess?" Mr. Dosher repeated. "You either did or you didn't."

"It wasn't on purpose," Rosie tried to explain.

"I see." Mr. Dosher took his index finger and pushed his glasses up the slope of his nose. Rosie had never noticed how long it was, because she had never talked to him face-to-face. "You mean, you were aiming for another part of her?" he asked.

It felt like a trick question to Rosie. She hesitated, and said, "I didn't aim. I mean, it just happened."

"Hitting someone doesn't just happen, Rosie. Violence is a deliberate act. There is always that split second when you can say to yourself, Do I really want to do this? Hit this person or steal this piece of candy?"

"I never stole candy," Rosie squeaked, wondering why she was defending herself against being a thief.

"Hitting, stealing, where does it stop? When your hand is raised, you have an opportunity to make the right or wrong choice. And I expect children in this school to make the right choice. Can you try and explain why the only solution you found to a problem was to hit a student?"

What could she say? That she'd liked Robbie forever and that Mary made her doubt herself time after time? Would it lessen her guilt and lessen her punishment? After some deliberation, Rosie said, "She told me she was sorry I ever existed."

Mr. Dosher blinked at her. " 'She was sorry you ever existed,' " he repeated. "Haven't you ever heard the words 'Sticks and stones can break my bones'?"

Sticks and stones may break my bones, but

words will never hurt me? Rosie would have rolled her eyes at Mr. Dosher if she'd had the nerve and wasn't scared to death. But words *did* hurt, she might have explained! Couldn't grownups see that? When her father left them and Rosie heard her mother say, "Please don't break up the family, Bob," his answer made Rosie burst into tears. "We haven't been a family for a long time, Lucy." Words don't hurt? What adult made *that* rule up?

"I'm sorry." It was all that Rosie could say. It didn't take away the hit, or the bloody nose, or the embarrassment she had felt when everyone watched her behave like a lunatic.

Mr. Dosher adjusted his glasses one last time. Rosie thought idly that his eyeglasses were nerdy but contacts wouldn't help him one little bit. "I'm glad you're sorry, Rosie, I really am. I'm sorry, too. But you're suspended. You can pick up your work in the morning and go to the detention room every day for the rest of the week. I want you to write an essay about what you did and why it was wrong. I'll be calling your mother to come and get you now. Is she at home?"

Rosie nodded and blinked back tears, fixating on the photo of the wet collie tongue. Mr. Dosher picked up the telephone, spoke to her mother briefly, and must have instantly ruined Mrs. Goldglitt's lunch. She was most likely eating a tuna fish sandwich, since she'd read that fish improved your memory. By the time Mr. Dosher hung up the phone, her mother was probably sick to her stomach.

Rosie left the office and weaved her way through throngs of whispering students, or was she imagining it? Were they pointing and jeering and gaping at her? Was she suddenly transplanted from a prison movie to a Western epic, where she had been taken captive and made to run the gauntlet, pelted by sticks and stones? Where was Lauren, and what about Summer, who didn't like Mary any better than Rosie did? Would they talk to her, a convicted criminal sentenced to detention? And what about Robbie? Could he bring himself to consort with a criminal?

Rosie jammed her books in her book bag and ran the gauntlet back to the bench outside the office, where sick children sat, waiting to be picked up by their anxious mothers. Rosie felt sick herself when she saw the flash of Mrs. Goldglitt's favorite red jacket appear at the door.

The look of anger on her mother's face was a hundred times more recriminating than Mr. Woo's sad eyes or Mr. Dosher's grim mouth. Stone-cold eyes and lips pursed together into a furious line for Rosie's joyride home.

Rosie's descent from the sky to the ground had been swift and fast, like a meteor's. She had started out Miss Rosie Goldglitt, in an excellent mood, that very morning. She was a crisp green leaf on a nice walk to school. For several hours, Rosie's name had matched her—golden, glittery; yes, life was good, to use Mr. Woo's favorite device, alliteration.

Why hadn't she remembered what Grandma Rebecca had once told her: all that glitters is not gold. Her new life was fool's gold, that's what it was. The Kissing Diary had fast become Rosie's Diary of Doom. She should never have retrieved it from the garbage can.

12

The Goldglitts at the Gynecologist

Mrs. Goldglitt walked swiftly ahead of Rosie and jumped into the car. She waited half a second for her daughter to close the door, and took off as if she had just robbed a bank.

"My seat belt!" cried Rosie before she understood that safety was not what Mrs. Goldglitt had in mind. Out of habit, she switched on the radio, and her mother turned it off. It reminded Rosie of Jimmy, but she didn't dare say so. She was afraid her mother might decide to drive the car into a ravine, if there *were* a ravine in the town.

"Is that all you have to say?" said her mother, which was confusing, to say the least, because Rosie hadn't said much of anything.

"I'm sorry," said Rosie, although a deep part of

her was not, the part that still throbbed from Mary's wishing that she didn't exist.

The air felt oppressive inside the car. Rosie opened a window, wondering if her mother's fury could give off heat.

"What on earth possessed you to hit someone, Rosie?"

She could barely hear her mother. Were her teeth clenched, preventing the words from escaping?

"Wait until I tell Dad."

Rosie couldn't believe what she was hearing. Her mother had cast her in an old-fashioned movie, except that the "Wait until your father gets home" routine was tired and pointless when your father didn't even live with you.

"She hates me," said Rosie.

"Who hates you? Dad's wife?"

"Dad's wife?" Rosie shouted. "Mary, that's who. Mary, the one that I hit, the one you told me was evil!"

"I may have said she was evil, but did I tell you to hit her? Did I, Rosie? Why on earth would you do that?"

"Because she hates me, and I hate her because she hates me, that's why!" So much for saying that she was sorry, but Rosie couldn't help herself.

Her mother sighed and turned her head slightly toward her daughter, as if she had switched on the air-conditioning inside her head. "You don't hit people because they hate you," she said, making an effort to soften her tone. "You ignore them, Rosie."

"If a baseball landed on your head, could you ignore it? If you stepped on a piece of glass, could you make believe you didn't, Mom?" Why hadn't she ignored Mary Katz? She'd done it for months and months and months. Why couldn't she be like Gandhi and turn the other cheek? She watched her mother drive past their street onto a major thoroughfare. It wouldn't do to complain.

"I can't believe this!" Her mother must have been thinking too hard, and was on the rampage again. "I need this, Rosie? With Grandma gone, and Grandpa sick, I need my own daughter behaving like a juvenile delinquent? Your father will blame it all on me, you know."

Rosie stayed silent. So *that* was the problem. Her mother was afraid she would be blamed for her downfall. Maybe it *was* her mother's fault that Rosie had screwed up. Maybe it was her father's fault, too, messing up their lives and leaving the family to marry someone else. Maybe Rosie was slugging the whole world, did her mother ever think of that?

"You'll have to come with me to the gynecologist's office," her mother said.

Rosie sucked in air. Just what she wanted, to be holed up in a room full of pregnant women.

They parked, and Rosie followed her mother into Dr. Shapiro's office, which smelled faintly of baby wipes and antiseptic.

"Sit," said her mother, tossing aside a copy of *Parents* Magazine that lay on the seat.

Rosie wedged herself between her mother and a woman whose belly was the size of the cage ball they used in gym when it was raining outside. She averted her eyes from the monstrous stomach.

Mrs. Goldglitt leaned across Rosie toward the woman, saying, "I hope you know that your baby could grow up and be suspended from school someday."

The woman smiled faintly and placed a protective hand on her belly, as if to say, Save us from this silly, raving woman. Rosie huddled in her seat, knowing that her mother was losing it and would embarrass her more before the visit was over. She grabbed a *Highlights for Children* and started leafing through it, hoping to find the tree with the hidden pictures, anything to distract her from her mother's lethal behavior. Rosie hid behind the magazine as if she were wearing blinders. She wouldn't look to the right of her where her mother had become a rattlesnake, nor to the left of her, where an alien was living inside a belly.

Mrs. Goldglitt found another target. Across from them, a mother was unstrapping a baby, cooing at her with such love that it made Rosie feel sad. Could her mother possibly have loved her as much as that? The baby had chubby round cheeks and a pink ribbon tied around a tiny strand of hair, which meant she was definitely a girl even if she looked like a boy.

"Yours, too," said her mother, startling the woman. "As cute as she is, she could grow up and be suspended from school someday."

"God willing," said the woman, unfazed by Mrs. Goldglitt. "Just let her be healthy." She hoisted the baby up and held her firmly in her lap, lifting her shirt up with the other hand. One, two, three, the baby was under it, latching on to the mother's nipple so quickly that Rosie was totally *mesmergusted* and *fascinpulsed*. She wanted to run out of the office and home to her bedroom, where she could call up Lauren and describe her horrible afternoon and hear her best friend laugh as if she hadn't hit Mary and gotten detention and ruined her life in an instant.

"Can I wait outside in the car?" Rosie hissed at her mother.

"Absolutely not."

Rosie's punishment continued as the baby sucked noisily. The hidden toys in the *Highlights* tree couldn't distract her. Terrific, thought Rosie, it was time for the other breast.

She made a note to herself never to nurse in public if there was a young girl around. She made a second note not to embarrass her daughter in a public place if she ever got suspended from school.

At last, her mother's name was called. "Just urinate in the cup, Lucy," the nurse said easily. Oh, joy and rapture, Rosie could sit there and imagine her mother peeing in a cup.

Finally, her mother returned to the waiting room. The nursing mother had gone and two more women in varying stages of pregnancy flanked Rosie, who had started reading *Working Mother* magazine out of sheer desperation. Mrs. Goldglitt paid at the glass window and muttered a thank-you.

"Come," she told Rosie.

In the car, Mrs. Goldglitt fastened her seat belt. She turned on the radio and let Rosie's music penetrate the air. "Sorry," was the first word she uttered.

"What?" said Rosie, stunned by the reversal.

"I should have dropped you at home. I don't know why I dragged you to the gynecologist."

"Do the crime, serve the time," Rosie answered. She was happy to hear her mother laugh for the first time all day.

Then Mrs. Goldglitt said, "Don't ever disappoint me like this again, Rosie. I don't ever want another phone call from the principal's office telling me that my daughter the hooligan is hitting some child."

Rosie considered her new nickname, *hooligan*, on the twenty-minute ride home. It was a far cry from hooking up with a boy named Robbie.

In her diary that evening, she gave herself several names. Her first choice, Rosie Gold-hitter, was to the point. Rosie Gold-bitter described her mood. The last one was signed:

Half-regretfully yours,
Rosie Gold-hooligan

13
Rosie's Intentions Did Not Include Detention

When they got home, Rosie's mother delivered her own set of detention rules: no television, no computer, no telephone. Rosie pleaded hard for her telephone privileges. How else would she know if her reputation was in the toilet? Her mother wouldn't budge.

"What was it you told me? Do the crime, pay the fine?" Mrs. Goldglitt said, raising an eyebrow.

Serving detention at home reminded Rosie of last year's blackout, except that she was the only one dealing with the misery of no electronics, and no one volunteered to play cards with her by candlelight. She did her homework, read a novel, and wrote a letter to her cousin in California, but she was itching to talk to Lauren and her friends.

Jimmy loped into the living room and tossed his

jacket over the easy chair, despite his mother's call from the kitchen to hang it up.

"Hey, slugger, how's it goin'?" he said, landing a few light punches on Rosie's arm. "I heard it on the grapevine that my sister's a thug."

"Very funny," said Rosie dejectedly.

"Hey, we all hit rock bottom sometime. I beat up Stanley Siddow in the eighth grade, remember?"

"That's true," said Rosie, brightening. Mrs. Goldglitt entered the living room and lifted up Jimmy's jacket with two fingers. "Hang it up," she said.

"Did you take away Jimmy's privileges when he beat up some kid in the playground?" Rosie asked her.

"Stanley Siddow was three hundred pounds and he sat on Jimmy's head and wouldn't let him get up," said Mrs. Goldglitt, unyielding. "It was self-defense. Besides, they separated the two of them, and Jimmy wasn't suspended. This is very different."

"Yeah, I'm going to jail," said Rosie.

"Detention sucks. I had detention when Mom and Dad were getting the divorce, and we were always getting to school late, remember?"

"You were late four times," said his mother. "And they made you stay after school."

"Whatever." Jimmy tossed his jacket back on the chair. "I've got my study group tonight. Can I hang it up later? What's for dinner?"

"Prison food," joked Mrs. Goldglitt. "Dry bread and water."

The following morning, Rosie sneaked a phone call to Lauren while her mother was in the bathroom. "Meet me at the rosebush where Robbie fell over," she whispered as soon as she heard her friend's voice. Rosie kept her eyes on the ground as she waited. She felt as though she were about to perform her Greek play all over again, except that this was her life and there were no extra rehearsals to make things better.

Lauren arrived looking very solemn. "Hey," she said as they headed toward the school.

"I'm so glad to see you," said Rosie, relieved, even if it felt as though she were going to a funeral.

"I called, you know. Your mom said you were grounded."

"We had bread and water for dinner," said Rosie, repeating her mother's joke.

Lauren didn't even smile. "Why did you do it?" she blurted out. "I know Mary bothers you, but did you have to hit her? What were you thinking?"

"Thinking had nothing to do with it," said Rosie. "I was out of control."

Lauren shook her head, and her sparkly barrette from Claire's Accessories threatened to come undone. "I was in a state of shock. I just couldn't believe you would do something like that!"

"You act like I planned it!" Rosie felt herself getting defensive. Couldn't Lauren support her instead of sounding like her mother? She lowered her voice. The way things were going, a rumor would circulate that she was yelling at her best friend and about to slug her. "I'm not saying it was the right thing to do, Lauren! What happened afterward?"

Lauren softened her own tone, saying, "I was at the nurse's office with Mary, so I missed a lot of it."

"What did Mary say?"

"That you were a threat to society and ought to be put away. That you should be expelled. The nurse put cotton in her nose, and it was all red. Mary kept saying, 'Is it broken? Is it broken?' Did you aim for her nose?"

"No," said Rosie, feeling a rush of shame. "It wasn't broken, was it?"

Lauren shook her head.

"It just happened," Rosie repeated. Punching someone in the nose was like a bad cartoon from the olden days. When was the last time she'd hit someone? When Jimmy had gotten angry and thrown her book bag out the door? All of her papers had scattered across the lawn, and Rosie had socked him, but not in the nose. Luckily, her mother had intervened, and Jimmy hadn't been able to punch her back. She pulled Lauren out of the main hall for privacy. "Does everyone think I'm a lowlife?" she asked.

"Just let it blow over and people will forget about it," Lauren said, looking around as though she was ready to bolt.

"What did Sarah say?"

Lauren's eyes flickered. "She said . . . what did she say?"

"Tell me."

"She said it was nuts!"

"Nice," said Rosie.

"Don't get mad! You know what you did was off the wall!"

Rosie could feel her face turn to stone. "And Summer? What did she say?"

Lauren put her hand out, as if it would make Rosie shut up. "Don't go through a list of people, please."

"Summer is not a list. Summer is Dumb and Dumber Summer who was tortured by Mary all through elementary school."

"She was . . . shocked." Lauren floundered. "She said it made you look bad and Mary look good."

Rosie felt herself go pale. "I guess she can't remember when Mary picked on her, and she didn't want to go to school, and her mother had to force her to go. Hey, maybe nobody wants to be seen with me anymore. I'm a . . ." Rosie cast around for the word she was looking for.

"An outcast?" said Lauren, trying to be helpful.

"A *felon*!" cried Rosie. Lauren looked confused, which didn't surprise Rosie, as she had always done better on vocabulary tests. "You're worse than my mother!" Rosie declared.

"It was *embarrassing*, Rosie! Can't you see that? It was like . . . *The Jerry Springer Show* or something!"

"I don't want to talk about it anymore," said Rosie, close to tears.

The bell rang and they hastily said goodbye, rushing away from each other so quickly that Rosie had no idea if they were friends or not.

As she walked in the direction of the detention room, the patter of feet and jingling chains made her think she was about to get mugged. "Rosie!" a voice called breathlessly.

Rosie turned around to see Teresa running toward her like a friendly dog.

"I just wanted to tell you that I'm in your corner!" said Teresa.

"What?" said Rosie, hoping it didn't look as though she was about to cry.

Teresa slung an arm around Rosie. "I'm not saying you should have hit her, but Mary has a new nickname now."

"She does?" said Rosie, trying to keep her eyes from welling up with tears.

"In gym class, somebody called her Bloody Mary, which has lots of connotations, if you know what I mean."

"Connotations?" said Rosie. Was that one of Mr. Woo's vocabulary words?

"I'm just saying that if they ever do a remake of the movie *Mean Girls*, Mary could be the star. You

138

stood up to her. Even if you did it the wrong way, Rosie."

"That means a lot to me," said Rosie, her voice husky.

Teresa took Rosie's arm and escorted her to the detention room as if she were squiring a princess. "Bloody Mary, that's her new nickname. She was the Queen of England for five years, so it didn't last much longer than middle school, you know? It's a drink made of vodka and tomato juice, too. My aunt had too many at my cousin's bar mitzvah. And Bloody Mary is the Polynesian lady from *South Pacific*. She's nasty, even if she sings some nice songs."

Rosie laughed. "Where do you get this stuff, Teresa?"

"See you later," said Teresa, patting Rosie's back and walking away, a cowboy with jingling spurs.

Rosie joined a dozen kids slouched behind their desks. They looked up to scrutinize each new arrival. Slipping into a chair behind Deena Corvo, who badly needed a dandruff shampoo, Rosie wondered what she'd done. Sworn at a teacher? Set fire to a wastepaper basket? Shown too much midriff, which, to judge by the outfit, might be the case? A teacher Rosie had never seen before waddled in, her billowing dress tent-like, camouflaging a large lumpy body. Rosie made a mental note to follow her mother's exercise regimen when she got older so that she wouldn't end up wearing tents.

"My name is Mrs. Caruso. Welcome to detention." She picked up a clipboard and read their names from a list, licking her finger as she turned the page. It reminded Rosie of her father, who licked his index finger when he was reading the newspaper. Germ-phobic Sarah said it was a nasty habit and made her feel sick. Her ex-friend Sarah, Rosie thought sadly.

"Billy Jones?"

Billy Jones? Rosie was astonished.

The door flew open and Billy hurtled through it. He mumbled a "Hi" and flopped into the vacant seat next to Rosie. Something was different about him that she couldn't figure out. "I'm here," he said.

"You're late," said Mrs. Caruso. "Here are the rules. You may do schoolwork or read a book. There will be no gum chewing, no eating, no headphones, no iPods. In other words, this is meant to be a punishment. It's not a vacation from school."

The minutes felt like hours. The hours felt like

days. Rosie memorized every chipped block on the wall. The hands of the clock moved incredibly slowly. By one o'clock, Billy's eyes were closed and he was snoring gently. The teacher rapped a paperweight on the desk and said, "No sleeping, either, Mr. Jones."

Billy blinked his eyes open and turned his head toward Rosie.

She smiled at him. "Why are you here?" Rosie whispered.

"Lateness," said Billy, smiling back. "How's your grandpa?"

"*No talking either!*" Mrs. Caruso said sternly, and Billy's mouth turned down as if he were a pouting child. Rosie tried not to giggle, certain that laughing wasn't allowed either.

When the final bell rang, Billy jumped to his feet and stretched his arms toward the ceiling, yawning noisily. He said, "That was a blast, wasn't it?" and left before Rosie could answer him.

The moment he was gone, she figured out what was different.

Billy Jones didn't smell anymore.

Rosie felt invisible when she hit the hallway. Grandma once told her that the older you got, the more invisible you became to the outside world.

When she got sick, Grandma made another discovery. Sick people became invisible, too. No one wanted to know them, or see them, or become them. If Grandma were alive, Rosie could tell her that she had found a new way to become invisible: punch someone in the nose and get detention.

Heads turned the other way and voices hushed as Rosie walked by. Summer was standing at Sarah's locker, and they were deep in conversation.

Rosie approached them with a breezy "Hey!" If she ignored the problem, maybe it would go away.

"Hey," said Summer, turning her back on Rosie and shutting her out. Sarah avoided looking at her altogether.

A lightning bolt hit her as Robbie rounded the corner, his familiar book bag with the Xbox logo slung over his shoulder. Summer and Sarah conveniently walked away, and Rosie called after them desperately, "Wanna hang out?"—the words nearly choking her. Overnight, it seemed they had lost their hearing.

"Hey, Robbie," said Rosie, and her heart registered a little bleep as his eyes made contact, until his face went dead.

Rosie wandered away, searching for Lauren, but she was nowhere to be found.

Then Rosie walked home, alone.

She went straight to her room and wrote in her diary:

Tuesday

Dear Diary,

I might as well be Grandpa with half a mind. I'm invisible. Lauren is mad at me. Sarah is Rosie-phobic, like I'm a snotty tissue. I hate to say it, but Summer is Dumb and Dumber Summer again, because she doesn't feel like being my friend anymore. All I can say is, <u>Bloody Mary!</u>

I am
Rosie Gold-bitterer-and-bitterer-and-bitterer

P.S. The only nice thing that's happened is that Billy is keeping me company in detention for lateness. So what does he do? He arrives there, late. News flash! Billy doesn't smell anymore. Wonder what happened.

Oh dear. My Kissing Diary has become a Dissing Diary, as in, I am dismissed.

14

Rosie's Intention Is to Never Again Get Detention

Detention was so boring that it made Rosie crave the classroom. Oh, what she'd give to solve a math problem, learn about the Aztecs, run after a ball in baseball, read a sonnet. Anything but stare at the back of John Lory's oily head, read for hours, count the dandruff flakes on Deena Corvo's shirt, listen to Billy snore, or wonder how many minutes would pass before Mrs. Caruso woke him up. When the bell rang announcing the end of the day, the students stood up in slow motion, as though they had lost every ounce of energy by focusing on nothing.

As soon as she saw Lauren, Rosie called out her name. "Lauren! Wait up!"

Lauren was slow to turn around.

"Where's everyone going?" Rosie said, joining the throng of kids heading down the hallway.

"The wrestling match. We're playing St. Christopher's."

Rosie tagged along hopefully, glad that no mention was made of yesterday's outburst. "I can't believe Summer and Sarah are ignoring me," she said. "What can I do?"

Lauren shrugged. "They'll come around. Bloody Mary is telling everyone that you're insane. And that her father might sue the school."

"Sue the school? My mother would freak, Lauren. I'd lose telephone privileges for a lifetime." Rosie sighed. She felt so low that it would take a gallon of chocolate ice cream and a thousand smiles in the mirror to make her feel better.

"Just get through detention," said Lauren. "Is Billy still there to keep you company?"

"He sleeps all day until the teacher wakes him up."

Rosie was delighted to hear Lauren laugh. Even if someone else was doing the laughing, it cheered her up. She followed Lauren into the gym, and they climbed up the bleachers, trying not to trip or step on fingers. Rosie had no wish to add to the humiliation of detention by taking a tumble and breaking her neck. Then again, if she ended up at the hospital, would it make people forget?

The gym was crowded, and in the distance they could see Sarah and Summer surrounded by kids, not a space in sight. Lauren settled into a vacant seat, and Rosie squeezed next to her.

"Is this the grownup section?" Rosie said, sizing up the adults wearing ugly sneakers and boring sweatsuits, a handful of businesswomen in dull suits and low heels, a smattering of men talking loudly about sports and the new condominiums being built.

"We're stuck," said Lauren. "We should have come earlier."

"I don't know anything about wrestling," said Rosie. "Do you?"

"I watched my cousin once. It's all sorts of moves you make to pin someone's shoulders to the ground. And then the referee bangs on the mat and gives the thumbs-up and another guy throws a towel onto the mat if the guy gets pinned." Lauren sat straight up and said in a mock whisper, "There's Tommy!"

"He's not going to hear you!" said Rosie, laughing.

"Shhhh!" said Lauren, smiling. "You never know!" There was a ripple of anticipation as the teams lined up.

The first pair of boys shook hands and circled around each other, the stronger boy swiping and lunging forward, grabbing at arms and legs until he had pulled his opponent to the floor. Rosie could feel her own neck muscles tense. Limbs made thumping noises and grunts erupted. They were present-day gladiators fighting until the end. Rosie held her breath so long that she had to force herself to breathe. The gym was dead quiet while the bigger boy pushed and pulled his opponent's limbs as if he were reconstructing a giant Pillsbury Doughboy. With a knee on one shoulder and trembling hands on the other, he held the struggling boy down until he lay still. The referee blew the whistle and the match was over. Rosie was exhausted.

The pinned boy got up, and shook hands with his opponent. Rosie looked at him curiously. He was about her brother's size, eyeglasses covered with a plastic guard, red-faced, sweating, a loser now. Although she had never seen him before in her life, Rosie felt a shock of recognition. The boy was pinned and helpless, struggling to free himself while the world was cheering his downfall. He

could have been Rosie except that he had played fairly and lost with honor. Rosie had simply lost.

A voice behind her brought Rosie back. A mother voice, saying, "Here comes my Robbie. I can't watch."

"What time is it?" said Rosie, pretending to look at the clock. The lady behind her had covered her eyes, leaving two fingers apart so that she could peer through the space to watch Rosie's crush lope onto the floor. *Robbie Romano's mommy,* thought Rosie as she scanned the faces of the rest of the team. There was Tommy Stone, hooting and hollering as Robbie faced a kid with a shock of blond hair and a concentrated meanness in his eyes that scared Rosie to death. Robbie was pinned and it was over before she could blink.

There was a murmur around her, like a low buzzing of bees, as the throng of wrestlers parted to let a lone figure weave his way toward the center of the gym where the referee waited. Stocky legs sticking out of shiny plastic pants, blue wrestling shoes with no cool logo, the usual mouth guard that made all of them look menacing. His hair was pulled back in a ponytail, which struck Rosie as odd because most of the sporty boys wore their hair short.

An Asian boy approached his wary ponytailed opponent. They shook hands, then circled and sized each other up. The Asian boy's face registered that he intended to murder; the ponytailed boy's eyes were tense and familiar.

"Who *is* that?" hissed Rosie, but as soon as the words were out of her mouth, she knew. Short? Yes. Sturdy? Yes. Boxlike? Absolutely. "Oh my God," she said at the same time as Lauren. "It's Teresa Tubby!"

Their eyes were riveted on Teresa's face as the Asian boy pulled her down. She wriggled like a pollywog out of water, flipping herself over so that her stomach was on the mat. The boy pulled and grappled in what seemed like desperation. Teresa settled her body and scrunched down hard, refusing to be moved despite more clawing and yanking. From their bird's-eye view, her breasts looked painfully squished together. It made Rosie wince, and she couldn't help wondering how the boy was feeling. Maybe he was brought up to honor women. To open jars for them. And car doors, too. To take out the garbage while his mother and sisters worked in the kitchen. Maybe he was brought up not to fight the opposite sex. To defend and protect them like they did in the olden days, before women could enlist in the army. To help ladies and children into the lifeboats first when the *Titanic* was sinking. Unless he was pretending that Teresa was a boy, or some person he hated, so that he could fight harder and ignore her girl parts more easily. Maybe he was angry that it was his hard luck to get stuck with a girl, the first girl anyone had ever seen on the wrestling team.

The people in the bleachers were going ballistic, screaming and whistling for their female wrestler. Rosie couldn't take her eyes off Teresa's face, grim and determined. A whistle signaled that the match was over, and Rosie thought, *Wow!* She wasn't pinned! But no, they had to fight each other again.

The wary circling began once more. They lunged and grunted, and Teresa managed to get on top of the boy, pushing at his shoulders, straining to keep him down. He rocked wildly and wrenched his body, throwing Teresa to the mat. When he scrambled to his feet, Rosie wondered if he was thinking, "No *girl* is ever going to pin me down!" But Teresa was relentless, flailing and lashing out like a wildcat. The boy lunged and swooped and took them all by surprise, knocking her down and flopping on top of her, pushing hard on her shoulders, his sleek boy biceps bulging from the effort.

Rosie watched with her mouth open, clutching Lauren's hand as if she were at the doctor's office getting a needle. Teresa was straining to keep her right side raised, but was forced to give up and give in and murmur a silent "Uncle," and the referee tossed the towel, signifying that the match was over.

"That had to hurt!" said Lauren, but Rosie could barely speak. She was so proud of Teresa she thought she would burst.

When the gym cleared of people, Lauren and Rosie straggled out.

Lauren ran to the bathroom while Rosie walked to her locker. She swung the door open, and a small folded piece of lined loose-leaf paper fluttered to the floor.

Before she could open it, she heard Teresa's voice. Tucking it into the pocket of her jean jacket, she went in search of her friend the female wrestler, Rosie's new idol.

Rosie found Teresa, wearing regular street clothes that were far from regular, a red shirt with a huge yellow smiley face on the front of it, a horrible orange-and-green pleated skirt that looked thirty years old, blue wrestling sneakers, and long black woolen socks. She was a sight to behold, cry-

ing out for the "don't" part of *Glamour* magazine's "Dos & Don'ts" page, but Rosie simply told her, "Congratulations!"

"Get with the program, Rosie Poo!" said Teresa. "I lost!"

"But you *did* it!" Rosie told her. "You, just you, against all of those boys, you know?"

"If you say so. Hey, maybe the next time you feel like socking someone, you should do it in wrestling." She gave Rosie a playful jab in the arm. She laughed and said, "You've gone through enough," which was a change for Rosie, as if she knew Rosie was wrong but stood by her anyway. "Hey, maybe sometimes you win when you lose, you know?"

Rosie hugged Teresa hard. "You're the greatest," she said, surprising herself by feeling it so fiercely.

"Thanks," said Teresa softly, adding, "I saw Lauren waiting for you in the main hall a minute ago."

Rosie searched the entranceway, but Lauren was nowhere to be found, so she walked home by herself, past the ice cream shop, which was empty enough for her to enter alone. Ordering a Blue Hawaii ice, Rosie felt better. Almost optimistic. Teresa had lost, but she was fine. Losing could be winning, like Teresa said. Rosie would get through detention and try to learn from her mistakes.

She sat at the back and licked her Blue Hawaii ice slowly, making up words for a new mantra. *Losing can be winning.* No, not quite. *Get over it, Rosie.* It didn't trip off the tongue. *Cute is okay, but smart is better.* She'd learned that too late. In the far corner of the shop, a girl with dark shiny hair was kissing the ice cream off her boyfriend's mouth. Rosie watched the scene as if it were a documentary in gym. The boy gripped the girl's neck, and it looked like he was strangling her. Rosie didn't like it, and made a note to herself: *Avoid the neck area, as it looks like murder.* The boy took the girl's head and turned it slightly, sticking his tongue in her ear. *Ewwww!* thought Rosie. *Earwax for dessert!* She made another mental note: *Clean your ears, just in case, or just say no.* Licking her ice as casually as possible, she pretended that she wasn't the least bit interested in watching them. The girl turned her head, and to Rosie's astonishment, it was Linda Reeves, Jimmy's girlfriend. Her eyes flew to the boy, but she knew her brother's shoulders, smaller and thinner. She knew his shaggy haircut, lighter in color. The boy looked older than Jimmy, and Rosie hated him immediately.

There was a jingle of bells and she half expected Teresa to appear, but a crowd of noisy boys entered the store. Rosie would have clutched at her heart had it not drawn attention, which was the last thing she wanted.

Robbie was among them, waiting at the end of the line, nearly reaching her table.

To Rosie's surprise, he didn't ignore her. "What's up?" he said, scanning the list of flavors. "There are too many choices. My brother likes Cotton Candy. Strawberry Shortcake sounds good."

She was grateful that he spoke, but was slow to answer, her Blue Hawaii ice cone up by her chin. She knew not to say to him that she was sorry he'd lost his match. "I had Black Cherry Cheesecake last time, and it was good." There. That wouldn't get her into trouble, would it?

"Cheesecake, huh? What about Mai Tai, what the heck is that?"

"I've got Blue Hawaii," said Rosie. "It's hard to choose."

One of the boys hollered, "Nice mouth, Rosie!"

Rosie was flummoxed. What had she said? Nothing smutty or gross, but they were shrieking with laughter.

Robbie ordered a butter pecan ice cream cone.

It figures, thought Rosie, who hated anything with nuts. He joined his friends outside, waving a hand as he left, not turning around with a smile or a nod. What did it mean, that she half existed? Rosie gave them time to get away, so that she wouldn't bump into them when she rounded the corner. She slunk home, confused.

Her mother was in the kitchen making coffee. She muttered hello to Rosie without looking up from her task. "How was your day?" she said. "I hope it was better than mine."

"Okay, I guess," said Rosie, not knowing where to begin. Did she tell her mother about Jimmy's girlfriend? About Robbie in the shop? About Teresa losing but winning her wrestling match?

"I started my day with a speeding ticket on my way to work. I must be slipping, Rosie, because as nice as I was to the officer, he gave me a ticket anyway." Mrs. Goldglitt was off and running before Rosie could say a word. "So this client at the beauty salon, an old lady who comes in once a week, tells me, You always look so sexy, with that beautiful figure, how do you do it? I'm feeling better, you know? Maybe the police officer was having a bad day, or something. She says, Do you exercise every day? I tell her I walk at least four times a week, and I use the elliptical trainer, and I thank her for the compliment, it's very flattering. Then she leaves, and Alice comes over . . ." Mrs. Goldglitt stuck her head inside the refrigerator. "Didn't I buy carrots the other day, Rosie?"

"I don't know, Mom. Finish the story."

"So Alice, you know Alice, a hairdresser at the salon, she comes over. She says, Doris was talking about you today. I say, I know, she asked me how I always look so sexy. Alice laughs, and says, No, she told me that a woman your age should dress appropriately, that you're not a teenager anymore, that you've got to be in your forties already. Can you imagine? I was ready to *spit*. Here she's complimenting me to my face and putting me down behind my back."

"Well, you are in your forties, Mom, but you dress fine. Even if I want to borrow your clothes. And you have a nice figure compared to most of the mothers."

Her mother poured herself coffee and sat down with a sigh, saying, "Thank you, honey. But it upset me so." She looked up at her daughter and cried, "Oh my God, what happened to your mouth?"

Rosie ran to the bathroom and looked in the mirror. Her lips and teeth were stained blue. "Nice mouth" was right! Rosie stuck out her tongue and it was aquamarine. She was a sight to behold. She called out to her mother, "No wonder they were all laughing at me in the ice cream shop! And Robbie was there! I can't stand it, Mom. What else can happen?" Back in the kitchen, she slumped into the chair and laid her head on the table. "My life is over."

Her mother reached over and stroked Rosie's head. "Are you dead? Are you hurt? Does it really matter if you have a blue mouth? It's kind of cute, you know?"

"Oh man," said Rosie, looking into her mother's somber brown eyes. "What about you, Ma? Look who's talking?"

"What about me?" she said, arching an eyebrow.

"Miss middle-aged teenager, what do you care what Doris thinks? Are you sick? Are you dead? Does it really matter?"

Her mother looked deep into Rosie's own green eyes that Grandpa used to tell her reminded him of emeralds. Finally, she said, "You're right. You're so right." Then she smiled slyly, and said, "Hey, let's not be *blue*!" and laughed so uproariously that Rosie had to join in.

"How could the policeman give such a beautiful mother a ticket?" said Rosie.

"How could anyone laugh at my adorable daughter, just because she has a blue mouth and tongue?" said Mrs. Goldglitt.

They laughed together some more, and without Rosie's even asking, her mother declared home detention officially over.

After supper, Rosie wandered upstairs to her room.

She wrote in her diary:

Wednesday evening

Dear Diary,

Today, Robbie laughed at me because my lips were blue. But I would have laughed at me, too, so I forgive him. Detention sucked, as usual, Billy slept all day and left right after. The best part was watching Teresa at the wrestling match. She blew me away! She's my new idol. Be yourself. Make mistakes. Rally. Mom and I had a few laughs, and I can watch television again, and go on the computer and make phone calls like a real person. Hurrah!

I have a dilemma. I saw Jimmy's girlfriend at the ice cream shop kissing somebody else. I don't understand it. When I saw Jimmy and Linda last week, they were all over each other. Today, she was all over somebody else. If I tell him, he'll hate me. If I don't, I'll feel awful. I'm going to wait and see if he says anything to me. So far, he hasn't. Maybe he doesn't know yet?

About kissing. I've set a goal for myself. I think if I kiss someone, I want it to be special, and only for him, not for anyone else. Otherwise, it's ruined. That's my theory right now. If Linda was practicing, she should have used a pillow, not another boy.

I am yours,
Rosie Goldglitt-turned-blue-but-getting-better

15

Rosie Goldglitt's Dance of Doom

*W*hen your father has a career in mental health, or as your mother puts it, in the "everyone is nuts" profession, it makes you watch what you say. Rosie did. If she told her father that she didn't like wearing green, he'd raise an eyebrow first. A ten-second pause would follow, and then the pursing of lips as he arrived at his psychological evaluation. Rosie might hear something like, "Your mother decorated your room in pale green when you were a baby, which I told her resembled the color of vomit. Perhaps this feeling goes back to infancy." If Rosie told her mother that she didn't like wearing green, her mother might say, "Wear purple. It brings out your eyes." Her father dug deeper than Rosie wanted. Sometimes, he was right, and the arrow hit the bull's-eye. Sometimes, it just made her crazy.

Rosie's father had been informed about the Hitting Episode the day it happened. To Rosie's relief, he couldn't make it to the house until Friday evening. Her mother was back to normal again and no longer considered her daughter to be a juvenile delinquent. All was forgiven, or at least forgotten. When Mr. Goldglitt entered the house, he shocked Jimmy by instructing him to go play Xbox. (Mr. Goldglitt believed that Xbox, PlayStation, and anything similar damaged social skills and killed off brain cells, even if he didn't know a thing about them. Rosie's mother worried less, but she hated the noise.)

Despite Rosie's protest that detention was over, at home and at school, her parents retreated with her into the kitchen, where they had a long discussion that she could have done without. Dad began by saying, "Your mother and I don't believe in hitting, anywhere, at any time. When you were a little girl and ran into the street, your mother slapped you out of fear."

Mrs. Goldglitt piped up. "You slapped her when she put her hand by the fire, remember?"

Rosie listened halfheartedly, and replayed the feeling she had had when Mr. Woo had looked at her so mournfully. Her father's expression reminded her once again that she had fallen off her pedestal and no longer possessed a shred of star power, whether she had served detention or not. The Goldglitt family didn't hit people.

Rosie suspected that her father took her out to dinner that very evening so that he could evaluate what made her "act out in anger," as he put it. Her brother begged off with a stomachache. Rosie didn't believe him. He had come home after school and flopped down on the couch, staring at the ceiling in a zombie state. Jimmy glared at Rosie when she gingerly asked him if everything was okay. He didn't look ill. He looked angry and hurt. Only Rosie knew why.

Mrs. Goldglitt's face darkened when she heard Jimmy was sick. She had made plans to go out to the movies with Sam. "Do you need me to stay home, honey?" she said to Jimmy.

"Nope," said Jimmy, still focusing on the ceiling.

Mr. Goldglitt put his hand on his son's forehead. "He might be a little warm," he said. "I don't think you should go out, Lucy."

Rosie's mother left the room.

Mr. Goldglitt followed, and they had a heated exchange. "He's a big boy!" said Rosie's mother.

"If he says I don't need to stay home, I believe him!"

"Get your priorities straight," said Rosie's father.

"They *live* with me. They're always my priority," Lucy hissed back at him. But guilt took over. She removed her coat, hung it up in the closet, and made a phone call to Sam.

"I don't think he's sick," said Rosie quietly. "I think he's sad."

Mr. and Mrs. Goldglitt snapped to attention. "Why would he be sad?" said Mrs. Goldglitt, alarmed.

Mr. Goldglitt was exhibiting his concerned therapist's face. "Has something happened to trigger a depression?"

"I saw his girlfriend kissing someone else."

"What girlfriend?" said Mr. Goldglitt, bewildered.

"Rosie saw him kissing a girl," said her mother. "He goes around the house singing."

"He did," said Rosie. "Her name is Linda Reeves. And a couple of days ago I saw her kissing someone else."

"Yikes," said Mr. Goldglitt, not sounding very therapeutic.

"The poor thing," said her mother. "I'm definitely not going out."

"See if you can get him to talk," said Mr. Goldglitt, calling goodbye to Jimmy as he and Rosie left the house. Jimmy didn't answer.

It was easier for Rosie to talk to her father while he was driving. She didn't have to look at his problem-solving face, his probing worried eyes, the hairs in his nose that needed trimming. He could make her so mad that sometimes she wondered if she had the same problems with her father that her mother did. The week before, when Mrs. Goldglitt had asked Rosie five times to get off the computer, she'd turned out the lights. Rosie typed in the dark until her mother pulled out the plug. Then she called Rosie's father on the telephone, saying, "Your daughter is being insubordinate again!"

Rosie took the receiver and said, "I don't even know what *insubordinate means*!"

"Sweetheart," Mr. Goldglitt started. "It means 'disobedient.' You have to listen to your mother, although it's very normal for someone your age to rebel. But every action has its consequences, and we'll have to punish you if it continues."

"We?" said Rosie. "What's the 'we,' Dad?

You're not even around to punish me. Don't you mean Mom?"

"I know you're speaking out of anger, Rosie. If you're talking about the divorce, sometimes the only person who can save your life is yourself. Even if it means sacrifices. I had to save my own life."

"So you sacrificed us," said Rosie coldly. Then she did exactly what her father had predicted. She rebelled by hanging up on him, and her mother had to call him back.

"What's with the 'we,' Bob, as in 'we' have to punish her? We haven't been a 'we' in a while, have we? I agree with Rosie."

"Lucy, it's only a figure of speech. We *do* have to enforce the rules and take control, before she's a full-blown teenager."

"If you ask me, she already is," said Mrs. Goldglitt. "It's only a matter of months."

"I'm what?" said Rosie.

"A full-blown teenager," said her mother.

Mr. Goldglitt decided that "he had to run," and the conversation ended.

When the almost full-blown teenager and her father drove to Angelo's for dinner that evening, her father spoke first. "So you saw Jimmy's girl-friend kiss somebody else?"

"Uh-huh," said Rosie. "It made me feel sick. Poor Jimmy. I think he liked her a lot."

"It's a rite of passage, having your heart broken."

Rosie didn't answer. Her father was right, of course. Maybe this was the year to have her heart broken. To never be kissed. To lose her good friends. To learn a lesson or two, even if she'd rather not.

"He'll survive," said her father. "I did."

"How was your heart broken?" Rosie asked. "You broke Mom's heart."

Mr. Goldglitt stopped at the traffic light. He bowed his head so that it almost rested on the steering wheel. "My heart was broken because I couldn't make it work." He changed the subject as the light turned green. "How are you doing, honey? You must be glad detention is over."

"My friends are acting weird," she said, praying that her father wouldn't say something stupid. She couldn't hang up on him, or jump out of the car in a strange neighborhood.

"You acted out of character." He turned into the parking lot. "The Rebel Rosie made them nervous. Do you think you want to talk to someone, professionally?"

"I'd rather not talk about it at all," said Rosie. "I'd rather talk about what I'm getting to eat. Spaghetti and meatballs."

Rosie's father chose the same, and a dish of broccoli rabe, her least favorite vegetable in the world. After all, her nemesis, Mary, liked it. She had looked up the word in the dictionary, and it fit Mary perfectly. Nemesis: the Goddess of Divine Retribution and Vengeance. Except Mary wasn't a goddess.

"Try it," said her father, offering her a forkful of the green stuff that made her want to puke. Rosie wrinkled up her nose, to which he responded, "Just say no thank you."

Was it a rite of passage to be embarrassed by your parents, Rosie wondered as her father chomped noisily on a piece of bread. She had left her mother at home, dressed in tight designer jeans for an evening out. Stiletto heels. A tiny top that most mothers would wear at least two sizes bigger.

"You're chewing too loudly," she whispered to her father, glancing nervously at the table next to them. She twirled her spaghetti and attacked it so fiercely that sauce splattered across her face.

167

Mr. Goldglitt kept eating, stopping only to compliment the food. Rosie couldn't find her napkin anywhere, and her father was using his to wipe his mouth. She was too shy to ask the waiter for another, and if she bothered her father, he would make her speak up. Then he would tell her that he just wanted her to learn to be more independent. Rosie would get defensive and say, "I'll learn that later."

She fished in her jean jacket for a handy tissue, and found one alongside the thin piece of loose-leaf paper folded into a square that she had forgotten to read. After cleaning her face, Rosie opened up the note. It was barely legible, but the way it was written, with no curlicues or flourishes, Rosie knew immediately that it was from a boy. She squinted at the scribble and read: "Would you like to go to the dance with me?" It was signed *R*.

Rosie felt just like Cinderella when the glass slipper fit and everything changed. The note had materialized and transported her to heaven. It neutralized detention and her annoying family. Her father's noisy chomping was music to her ears. Her brother's sullenness didn't pain her anymore. Her mother could dress as skimpily as she wanted.

Rosie knew in her heart that she would be Mr. Woo's star again. Lauren and her friends would come back to her. All was forgiven. Life glistened like a jewel. Robbie Romano had asked her to the dance.

Rosie shared a dish of zabaglione with her father to celebrate. He quizzed her in the car about how she knew Robbie. Oh, this is the boy who fell over in the bushes? Who said you were cute in the play I didn't see? Who didn't talk to you for a while after you insulted his manhood? (That one hurt.) Didn't he have the courage to ask you in person? Is he so intimidated that he had to write a note? Is he the son of the man who crashed into your mother's car? On any other day, Rosie might have exploded, but the note, nestled in her pocket like a diamond, had granted her tranquillity.

When they got home, her mother was washing the kitchen floor.

"Is everything okay?" said Mr. Goldglitt.

"What do you mean?" said Mrs. Goldglitt, squeezing out the mop.

"You're cleaning!" he said, enjoying his own joke.

"Don't quit your day job to become a comedian," said Mrs. Goldglitt. "How was dinner, Rosie?" She brightened at the sight of her daughter's face. "You're beaming!" she said.

"I am?" said Rosie, handing her the note. Her mother started hunting for her reading glasses and held the paper to the lamp when she couldn't find them.

"Never mind," said Rosie, tucking the note in her pocket. "Robbie asked me to the dance!"

"No kidding!" cried her mother, dancing a jig with the mop.

"Your mother was always a good dancer," said her father, smiling.

Mrs. Goldglitt laughed, surprising Rosie.

Rosie left her parents talking pleasantly in the kitchen. She wanted to go upstairs and read the note in her bedroom. Examine every ink splotch. Hold the paper to the light. See if he'd somehow drawn an invisible heart.

Jimmy called to her from the living room. "What happened?" he said. He was still on the couch, but he was watching television.

"Robbie asked me to the dance." She perched next to him, hoping he wouldn't burst her bubble.

"That's good," said Jimmy. "I hope you have fun."

Rosie looked at her brother. His eyes were full of pain, as if the rite of passage that her father had talked about had damaged him. "Are you okay?" she asked him.

"I guess," said her brother. "We only lasted three months. Linda and me."

"She was pretty," said Rosie, not knowing what to say.

"She still is," said Jimmy. "She's just not . . . mine. I mean, she never was. But I felt so good when I was with her."

Rosie took his hand, and Jimmy actually let her hold it for three or four seconds. They spent the rest of the night watching television together. Brother and sister, side by side. Rosie even kissed him good night, and he didn't push her away or pretend to rub it off.

Later, in bed, Rosie wrote in her journal:

Friday night

Dear Diary,
Things have changed. This may become a kissing diary after all. Robbie asked me to the dance! I have nothing to wear, and I hope Mom will take me to the mall to buy a dress, and not

complain about money. Today I discovered that grownups have it hard, maybe as hard as we do. I didn't fight with Dad, and my mom was so happy that Robbie asked me out she danced with a mop. You had to be there.

I'll have to speak to Lauren about what she's wearing. I don't even know if she's going, I realize. This week in detention was terrible. I lost touch with the world!

I'm kissing this page, wearing my new lipstick . . . in case it happens!

Lots of love,
Rosie Life-glitters

P.S. Jimmy's recovering from a broken heart. I love my brother. If he reads this, I'll deny it.

16
Rosie Goldglitt, Smitten

Rosie was up early on Saturday morning. She couldn't stay in bed, thinking about the dance and Robbie and what would they talk about and would she find something pretty to wear when her mother took her shopping?

"Can't we go to the mall tonight, Mom, right after work?" Rosie interrupted her mother, eating her last piece of whole wheat waffle.

"I'm seeing Grandpa tonight, honey, but I promise I'll take you tomorrow." Mrs. Goldglitt gulped down the rest of her coffee. "Now let me go so that I can make some money."

"I can get shoes, too?" Rosie asked.

"Absolutely. Where are my car keys? Sam says I should put a hook on the wall so that I'll always know where they are."

"I saw them in the dining room." Rosie smiled. "A hook is a great idea, Mom, but only if you remember to put them there."

"True," said Mrs. Goldglitt, laughing. Her face became serious. "Do you want to come with me to visit Grandpa?"

"I should," said Rosie. "Shouldn't I?"

"It would be nice," said her mother. "I'll pick you up after work. Ask your brother when he wakes up."

Visiting Grandpa at the nursing home was a somber affair. Rosie's heart beat quickly as they entered the building. The nurse directed them down a corridor to the game room, where they found Grandpa slumped over in a wheelchair with his chin on his chest.

"Is he sleeping?" whispered Rosie.

Jimmy crouched down so that he could see. "His eyes are open."

"Hi, Dad," said Mrs. Goldglitt, sounding falsely cheerful.

"Hi, Grandpa," Rosie said. "This is the game room?" she whispered to Jimmy, looking around. Not a single person was playing Parcheesi or Mo-

nopoly or Uno or anything resembling a game, although the shelves were stacked with them.

"Sometimes I've seen them stringing beads," said her mother. "Daddy," she said, stroking her father's cheek.

He lifted his head, and for a moment his eyes seemed to register something, a glimmer of recognition, a connection. Confusion followed. He looked straight past his daughter and beyond Rosie, his eyes settling on Jimmy.

"Harry?" he said, one hand rising in what was almost a wave. "Harry!" he repeated, his voice cracking.

Mrs. Goldglitt bent down so that her eyes were level with her father's. "That's Jimmy, your grandson," she said clearly.

"Who's Harry?" Jimmy asked.

"His brother Harry. He died when Grandpa was a little boy," said Mrs. Goldglitt, patting her father's arm. "Harry fell out of a tree, didn't he? It was a long time ago, wasn't it, Pop?"

"Great," said Jimmy. "He sees dead people."

"At least he's calling you something," Rosie said. "He won't even make eye contact with me, Jimmy."

"Harry," said Jimmy. "Call me Harry."

Mrs. Goldglitt sighed. "He has good days and bad days, and the bad days are taking over. I'm sorry, children." She looked at her watch. "It's too late to take him out to the garden. Do you want to see where he sleeps?"

They wheeled Grandpa out of the game room and down the hallway into a room with a bed, a desk, a chair, a dresser, and a sink. Rosie and Jimmy exchanged glances. Jimmy coughed, uttering the word *prison*.

Mrs. Goldglitt stationed Grandpa by a small table with a cluster of frames on it. "These are pictures of all the people who love you, aren't they, Pop?"

They no longer expected Grandpa to answer. Rosie said, "The bed is so tiny! Didn't he and Grandma buy a king-sized bed so that he had plenty of room for his feet?"

"Honestly, honey, I don't think he knows much of anything now."

"We used to jump on it, didn't we, Rosie?" Jimmy spoke close to Grandpa's ear. "When we were little, we had fun jumping on your bed!"

Grandpa grunted.

"Do you remember?" said Rosie in a small voice.

He dipped his head down so that his chin was on his chest again.

"I think I'm ready to go," said Jimmy, heading for the door.

"Wait," said his mother. "Dad, do you want to sit in front of the television set before it's time for bed?"

Mrs. Goldglitt turned him around and pushed the chair back down the hallway to the television room. The three of them took turns kissing him goodbye.

"Come again," said the nurse as they passed the main desk. "He was happy to see you."

Jimmy pushed open the heavy doors to the outside world. "How could she tell?" he said, astonished.

Rosie and Jimmy started laughing hysterically, and Rosie said, "We're sorry. We're sorry! We can't help it!"

"It's okay," said her mother. "It's better than crying."

They walked a few blocks to the Italian restaurant nearby, and ordered eggplant heroes. Nobody talked much, although Rosie was tempted to bring up their imminent shopping spree.

When the heroes arrived, Rosie took her sandwich and held it in the air. "To Grandpa," she said.

"To Grandpa," said Jimmy, taking a quick bite and raising his own.

"Don't get tomato sauce on the tablecloth," said Mrs. Goldglitt, smiling.

On Sunday morning, Rosie telephoned Lauren to see if she could come shopping with them. According to Mrs. Jamison, she was sick in bed. Rosie hoped the story was true, and not just an excuse to avoid her altogether. Summer and Sarah were nowhere to be found, but nothing could shake Rosie's good mood as she and her mother got into the car. Her mother made the comment "I hope this dance doesn't cost me a fortune," to which Rosie replied, "I can raid my piggy bank."

"Bloomingdale's is out," said Mrs. Goldglitt, but Rosie couldn't help noticing the excited glint in her mother's eye that shopaholics get before a spree. Next to a great cup of coffee and her boyfriend, Sam, nothing put a smile on Mrs. Goldglitt's face the way shopping did. Buying for her daughter was almost as rewarding.

Mrs. Goldglitt was elated when they found a dress in the mall that was inexpensive enough to keep the glint in her eye. It was short, fruit-free, a soft violet color that brought out Rosie's eyes, and she felt downright pretty wearing it. They found a cheap little matching beaded handbag, a pair of low strappy heels, and dangling fake diamond earrings that her mother wasn't sure about.

On Monday morning, Rosie's eyes were bright and shining as she talked about the pretty outfit they'd bought. "I hope Robbie likes it!" Rosie said, munching on Cheerios although it was a junk-food cereal day.

"You're smitten, I can see," said Mrs. Goldglitt.

"What does that mean?" said Rosie, smiling from ear to ear.

"How do I explain it?" Mrs. Goldglitt ran to the unabridged dictionary, which she kept under the china cabinet in the dining room. "It says, 'struck hard.' So when I say it, I mean, struck hard by love! Remind me to vacuum someday," she added, brushing the dust off the book's cover.

"You're not smitten by vacuuming," Rosie said, making her mother laugh.

At school, Lauren was nowhere to be found.

Rosie bumped into Summer at her locker. "Is that the lip gloss we bought together?" she said, hoping that going back to normal would make everyone forget about the past.

"I don't think so," said Summer uneasily. "It's Pink Meringue." Her eyes wandered away from Rosie.

"It looks pretty," said Rosie. "Have you seen Lauren?"

"She still has the flu," said Summer, slamming her locker and turning to leave.

"She's been sick forever!" said Rosie, putting out her hand. "Summer! Can we talk?"

"About what?" Summer said cautiously.

"Are you mad at me or something?" Rosie couldn't help saying what was on her mind. "I mean, are you Mary's friend now? I'm not saying it was right what I did," she added quickly.

"Can't we just forget about it, Rosie?"

"I'd like to. But things are funny between us, you know?" Her voice caught in her throat.

"It's just that . . ." Summer searched for the words. "How do I put this? Mary tortured me every day. You were in my class, remember?"

"But that's what I'm saying! Why are you so upset with me?"

"Let me finish. Mary told everybody that I smelled. That I didn't know how to read, which made it awful when we went around the class and had to read out loud, because I got so nervous and stumbled more, and I was a good reader, Rosie! Dumb and Dumber Summer, remember? She told people not to invite me over to their house! And a lot of them didn't! It was the worst year of my life."

"I know that," said Rosie, her voice low. "Then why shut me out?"

"She was way worse to me, and I never did a thing. I never talked to anyone about it, and my mother didn't either. She made me go to school, like nothing was happening. She told me to try and be nice to her. Can you believe that? Do you know, I brought her a candy bar one day? One of those huge Hershey bars? She sniffed it and made a face, and threw it right in the garbage can, in front of everyone. So maybe I'm mad because I didn't do anything. And you did."

"I'm sorry, Summer. I didn't realize."

Summer's lip was trembling. "And do you know what your hitting Mary did? It just made everyone feel sorry for her. I don't remember anyone feeling sorry for me when I didn't want to get out of bed in the morning to go to school. When I wanted to crawl into the closet and stay there forever." A tear spilled down her cheek.

"I'm so sorry," Rosie repeated, her own eyes welling up. "But I know what you were feeling. All week, I wanted to crawl into the closet and stay there forever." She paused for a moment, and said, "Do you really think people feel sorry for her? That makes me want to puke."

"I hope not, that's for sure. Are you crying?" Summer brushed the back of her hand across her eyes. "Don't get me started. A secret part of me is glad you did it. Payback time. But not that way, Rosie, you know?"

"I know." Rosie took a chance, holding out her arms to Summer. Summer moved into them, and they hugged each other hard. "I'm glad we talked," Rosie whispered.

"Me too," said Summer. "I feel better. And Sarah will come around, I promise."

By the time they said goodbye, Rosie realized that she'd forgotten to tell her about Robbie. When Rosie opened up her locker to get a few books for class, another white note floated to the floor. This time she opened it immediately. It said, "Meet you at the famous rosebush, seven-thirty."

All smiles, Rosie walked into homeroom. She chatted with her friends, never mentioning detention. Teresa was her usual friendly self, and seemed less like an outsider to Rosie. Even her clothes looked more acceptable. Who cared if her pink shirt didn't match her red plaid skirt? On Teresa, somehow, it worked. It occurred to Rosie that perhaps she was the one who had changed.

As soon as Rosie entered English class, Mr. Woo called her over to the desk. "Welcome back, Rosie," he said quietly.

"Nothing like that will ever happen again," she said.

"I know that," said Mr. Woo, winking at her.

The wink meant everything. She sat down at her desk, turning quickly around to smile at Summer. Then she leaned toward Robbie and said, "That's fine."

He answered, "Okayyyyy," drawing out the word. It was enough for Rosie.

As soon as she got home, Rosie called Lauren. "I'm still sick!" her friend croaked. "You sound happy! What's up?"

"I am!" said Rosie. "But not that you're sick! Robbie asked me to the dance. Can you believe it?"

"That's great!" said Lauren. "I'm so bummed,

because I never got the nerve up to ask Tommy Stone! Summer and Sarah are going with me, if I'm better by Friday."

"You'll be better, it's four days away!"

"I'm staying home tomorrow, and if I don't have any fever, my mom says I can go in on Wednesday. I miss you!"

Rosie hung up the phone, a huge smile on her face. She and Summer were friends again. Sarah had said goodbye to her today, and had even given her a hug. It was funny how happiness was something that was better when you shared it with your friends.

On the day of the dance, Robbie and Rosie exchanged glances only. It was as if the act of going together had made them both so nervous that they could no longer speak. Rosie raced home to get ready, four hours early. She shampooed her hair and toweled it dry. Her mother would style it for her later, with the curling iron that she'd brought home from the salon. Mrs. Goldglitt had watched Jessica at work making soft ringlets on several clients already.

Rosie sat down at the computer and looked up Robbie Romano under his screen name. What had she heard him tell his study group his name was? RobRom15.

She scanned his profile.

Name: People call me Robbie, and my parents call me Robert when they're mad at me. Rosie thought it was brave of him to mention his parents. Who cared?

Location: In my room playing Xbox Live, or in my driveway shooting hoops. Rosie wasn't surprised by Robbie's love for Xbox. Jimmy played it, when his homework was done. She could hear strange boys shouting in the living room from all over the country! Rosie made a note to ask Jimmy which games he liked so that she could mention them to Robbie. She wouldn't be fake and pretend that she played them, but at least it would provide a few minutes of conversation.

Gender: Male. No kidding, thought Rosie. What were the rules? Don't insult their egos. Don't ask if you scared them. Don't eat Blue Hawaii ice or hit someone in the face or do anything embarrassing. It made them clam up.

Hobbies and Interests: Hanging out with friends, Xbox Live, music by Sublime, the comedian Dane Cook.

Rosie ran into Jimmy's room and found one of

his Sublime CDs. She read the liner and the lyrics from top to bottom and played the music while she researched Robbie. Music was safe to talk about. What did she have now? Sublime, Xbox, Dane Cook. About three minutes of conversation, but it was a start.

Rosie looked in the mirror and formed her lips into a pout. Would Robbie kiss her? Who knew? Would she like it? Maybe. Would he know where their noses were supposed to go? She hoped so. Would she be the first girl Robbie kissed? In a way, it would be easier if he was a virgin kisser. If there was no competition, Rosie could be the best, but she could also be the worst. But if he knew how to do it, Robbie could show her. She was a fast learner. She picked up Spanish easily. And dance steps, too. Why not kissing? Rosie laughed out loud.

A half hour before she was supposed to meet Robbie at the rosebush, the famous rosebush where he had fallen over backward, Rosie was dressed and ready to go. She made a last-minute call to Lauren, who picked up the phone and said, "Hey, we miss you! We're all getting ready at my house."

Before Rosie could feel bad that she hadn't been

invited, Summer grabbed the phone. "Don't kiss anybody before we get there, okay? We'll see you inside."

Rosie started to laugh. "Hey, I promise! What did we decide? Leave the lip gloss on or take it off?"

"Eat something inside, and it will come off on its own. Then you won't have to decide," said Summer, laughing. "Break a leg!"

Sarah picked up the phone. "Summer thinks it's a play or something! I'm not kissing anyone. It's germ season, you know."

Rosie heard Summer say, "It's always germ season for you, Sarah!" to a chorus of laughter.

"I'm nervous!" Rosie said, wondering if anyone was still on the phone.

Lauren was back. "Don't be!" she said cheerfully. "We'll be there to rescue you if you need any help!"

Mrs. Goldglitt started screeching about how late it was getting, and to brush her teeth and get her coat. "You're not the one going, Mom," said Rosie.

"I'm as nervous as a cat!" said her mother, examining her daughter from head to foot, and rubbing Rosie's face with a tissue. "Too much blush.

You look like Grandma Rebecca's porcelain doll with all that rouge. But Grandpa would tell you that you looked beautiful, honey. If he were here."

"Better than cute," said Rosie softly, feeling a wash of sadness pass between them.

When they arrived at the school, Mrs. Goldglitt didn't want to let her out of the car. "I can't leave you here alone," her mother protested, but Rosie convinced her that a yardful of students would keep her safe. "Be good," she said, leaning over to kiss her. "Have fun, be smart, don't drink or drive."

"What?" said Rosie, in mock protest. "I was going to drive Robbie to the beach afterward!" She made a face and said, "And drink? What are you thinking? It tastes worse than coffee!"

"Good," said her mother, smiling broadly. "I'll pick you up at eleven."

When she was gone, Rosie's heart started hammering as if she'd run the track three times. She was scared and eager, and excited, too. What could she call it? *Sceager* sounded right.

Rosie found the rosebush that had made Robbie fall over backward. The famous rosebush where it had all begun. It was getting darker now, and the front of the school was deserted. Maybe her mother was right. She should have stayed in the car until she'd spotted Robbie. Rosie shifted from foot to foot, peering into the distance, searching for Robbie's lanky frame.

A voice made her jump. "I saw him over there, on the other side of the school, by Mrs. Petrie's house!"

Rosie squinted her eyes in the darkness and saw the glint of a hundred buttons. It was Teresa Tubby, her girl Teresa, top wrestler and true friend, her eyes trained on Rosie. "There's a rosebush on the other side of the school, you ninny!"

Rosie ran like a maniac, following her heroine past the front steps of the school, past the flagpole, past the sign that said SEVENTH GRADE CAR WASH ON SATURDAY. In the distance she saw two people, a boy and a girl. The girl had long blond hair that shimmered in the streetlamp. The boy's hair was spiky, and his face was in shadow. Robbie and Mary. Mary and Robbie. She could have spotted them anywhere, her crush and her downfall. The kiss exchanged between them was a knife in Rosie's heart, and she stepped back quickly, trying to save herself from falling.

The noise startled the two of them, and made them look up.

Robbie's mouth hung open. Mary followed his stare and said, "Can I help you, Miss Peeping Tom?"

Teresa reappeared with Billy in tow. He reminded Rosie of her cousin's golden retriever, coming to rescue the damsel in distress.

"Hey," said Billy, and Rosie mumbled something back. "I've been looking for you! Weren't we supposed to meet at Mrs. Petrie's rosebush? The one I thought your grandfather was looking for? Teresa said you were waiting by the other rosebush!" He held out his hand, and Rosie took it gratefully.

Teresa took Rosie's other arm, and said out loud, "You know he got detention defending you!"

Rosie glanced sharply at Billy, who smelled only of aftershave and was her second newest hero. "I thought you said you were in detention because of lateness," she said.

"I lied," he said shyly, and they turned the corner and entered the fiesta-decorated gymnasium without looking back.

"I forgot there was more than one rosebush," Billy whispered. "I thought you'd remember."

"Detention got my memory," Rosie fibbed. "Mr. Woo would be proud. You used symbolism!"

"Too bad we met at the wrong symbol, huh?"

"And your handwriting sucks," Rosie scolded him gently.

She would never tell Billy that his *B* looked like an *R*, especially when she had wanted it to be so. Teresa had saved her, with her jingling chains and her hundreds of buttons and her heart of gold. Rosie would tell her other friends, Lauren, Summer, and Sarah, that they should take her blunder and put it in the vault and never speak of it again. She would never ever tell, cross her heart and hope to trip backward over a blooming rosebush.

17

Rosie's New Mantra

ater in the evening, sitting on a bench under one of the piñatas, Rosie discovered that she could say anything she liked to Billy. She didn't have to run home and log on to the computer to look up his profile. Rosie even apologized for those times she held her nose. "I feel terrible about it," she said, looking to see if he was insulted.

To her relief, Billy laughed and said, "Hey, I deserved it! We have Teresa to thank for conquering my hygiene problem. If she hadn't told me, you'd still be holding your nose! It's hard to catch a whiff of yourself."

It seems that the Tubby family had moved next to the Joneses a few years back. They were friendly neighbors. Following Rosie's discussion with Teresa Tubby about Billy's odor, Teresa had taken matters into her own hands. She had rung his doorbell and dragged him into the kitchen in what might have felt alarmingly like a wrestling move. She didn't hold back, telling him, "Consider me an intervention of one."

"What's an intervention?" Billy had asked her, mildly confused.

"If you were doing drugs, your family and friends would be here to tell you that you're ruining your life."

"I don't do drugs," said Billy, mystified.

"If you drank, we'd be saying the same thing."

"Does milk count?" Billy asked, still clueless.

"You smell," said Teresa matter-of-factly. "You need help so that you don't drive all your friends away."

And that was that, Billy told Rosie. He was an only child whose parents had divorced when he was a little boy. Billy never bothered to ask his mother when to use deodorant. He thought you were supposed to put it on after physical exertion. Following gym class, sweating profusely, Billy put on his deodorant and went to class. The rest was history.

They talked until they got thirsty, and left the bench to get a cup of punch. Tommy Stone's mother accosted them both. "You're the only kids that haven't been photographed tonight!"

She led them to a booth that was covered in shiny blue paper. Silver stars hung from ribbons fixed to the top. Sitting them down, she whispered to Rosie, "How did a nice girl like you end up slugging Mary Katz?"

Rosie shrugged, and felt her cheeks turn red, but when Mrs. Stone turned to get her camera, Billy coughed into his hand, muttering, "Loser."

"Can you believe it?" whispered Rosie. "Tommy Stone must have told his mother!"

"*Gossip Girl*!" said Billy, which surprised her, as most boys didn't know the names of books that girls read.

Mrs. Stone took their picture, and the two of them stayed talking inside the star-festooned box. It was nice and secluded, and Rosie didn't feel a moment of shyness. Index cards were not necessary when it came to Billy.

Rosie asked him, "Didn't you mind when people made fun of you? I get upset, because I want everyone to like me, you know?"

Billy laughed, and said, "Not everybody likes me, that's for sure. And if I knew how bad I smelled, I'd hold my nose, too!"

Rosie felt something hit her on the back of her head. Had Mary Katz secretly crawled behind the booth to torture her? No, it was a star made out of heavy cardboard, knocking her on the head and falling to the floor.

"It didn't hurt you, did it?" Billy asked her.

"No," she said, touched by the concern in his voice. "The attack of the shooting stars!"

Billy picked up the star and twirled it in the palm of his hand. He handed it to Rosie, and said, "You've been my star for a while." It was Billy's turn for his cheeks to turn red.

Then he leaned toward Rosie and kissed her once, very gently. Their noses didn't bump. Their teeth didn't clink. Fireworks didn't explode the way they did in the movies, but she liked the kiss. What was the word for it? *Sweet*, she thought. Close to tender. Were there stars in the air? Just cardboard ones, dangling above her. But Billy had called her his "star for a while," and had kissed her to prove it. For an instant, she pictured Mary kissing Robbie at the rosebush, the bush where Robbie had fallen over backward. Let them fall over backward to-gether, thought Rosie. She no longer cared. Just like that, Robbie Romano had turned into a shooting star of his own and flown out of Rosie's heart.

Maybe life had to do with finding a new constellation. Teresa, unique and so original, had turned into Rosie's dearest new friend. Billy, supporting her through thick and thin, was a planet that Rosie had just discovered.

Lauren came over and didn't seem surprised to see her friend sitting close to Billy. She leaned down and whispered in Rosie's ear, "You look cute together!"

Rosie rolled her eyes and said, "Don't use that word in front of me, please," which made both of them laugh. A shared secret between two best friends.

Billy waited outside with Rosie for her mother to arrive. She pulled up to the curb at 11:05 and watched Billy give her daughter a peck on the cheek before she got into the car.

"Whatever happened," her mother said, "you still look happy."

"I am," said Rosie, surprised by her calmness. "Did you recognize Billy?"

"Of course," said her mother. "He's such a good boy."

Rosie smiled. "He is," she said. "I think he's smitten."

"Why wouldn't he be?" said Mrs. Goldglitt. "Which reminds me that I have to vacuum tomorrow."

"Or the dust bunnies will gather, and Sam will make fun of you."

Her mother laughed, and shook her head. "Dad would have liked it if I'd kept a cleaner house," she said.

"But then you would have been perfect!" said Rosie, happy to hear her mother's laughter.

The porch light was shining when they pulled into the driveway. Rosie caught a glimpse of her brother at the window. She walked into the living room, where he was sitting on the couch, legs on the coffee table as if he'd been lounging there for a while.

"Boys are weird," she said amiably.

"So are girls," said her brother.

"Wait till you're grown up," said Mrs. Goldglitt. "It gets even stranger."

"Good night," said Rosie, floating upstairs in a haze of happiness.

She took out her diary and found the next clean page.

Rosie wrote:

At last I can say, This is my Kissing Diary.
The following is a poem, which is not about
Robbie.

Roses are red,
Violets are blue,
Sugar is sweet,
And Billy Jones is, too.

I had a great time at the dance, even if I got
my boys and my rosebushes all mixed up.

I had my first kiss, and I'm glad it happened
with Billy. It makes sense to get kissed by someone who really likes you. The funny thing is, I
like him back. He's such a good boy, as my
mother says. And I can honestly say that he's a
good kisser, too. I wonder if I am? I think if
you like someone it makes the kissing better, but
that's only my opinion, with very little experience.

I still don't like Mary. I probably never will.
She was kissing Robbie, and it hurt a lot. I
wonder if she did it to get back at me? It doesn't
really matter. Teresa arrived, and then Billy came
along. We had the best time ever!

I've been thinking a lot about my name. It's not so bad. Mr. Woo handed me a sheet of quotations by Shakespeare. He highlighted this one:

<u>What's in a name? that which we call a rose</u>
<u>By any other name would smell as sweet.</u>

I think it means that if I'm a nice person, my niceness will shine through no matter what my name is. So Rosie Goldglitt may sound dorky, but I'm not.

I'm really tired. I'll write more later. Meanwhile, I'll sign myself plain old

Rosie Goldglitt

P.S. I've thought of a new mantra. <u>Life is what you make it, Rosie Goldglitt.</u> It kind of rhymes, doesn't it?
P.P.S. I've taped my falling star above my dresser. I like being a star.